Gustave Flaubert

was born in Rouen in 1821, the son of a prominent physician. A solitary child, he was attracted to literature at an early age, and after his recovery from a nervous breakdown suffered while a law student, he turned his total energies to writing. Aside from journeys to the Near East, Greece, Italy, and North Africa, and a stormy liaison with the poetess Louise Colet, his life was dedicated to the practice of his art. The form of his work was marked by intense esthetic scrupulousness and passionate pursuit of *le mot juste;* its content alternately reflected scorn for French bourgeois society and a romantic taste for exotic historical subject matter. The success of *Madame Bovary* (1857) was ensured by government prosecution for "immorality"; *Salammbô* (1862) and *The Sentimental Education* (1869) received a cool public reception; not until the publication of *Three Tales* (1877) was his genius popularly acknowledged. Among fellow writers, however, his reputation was supreme. His circle of friends included Turgenev and the Goncourt brothers, while the young Guy de Maupassant underwent an arduous literary apprenticeship under his direction. Increasing personal isolation and financial insecurity troubled his last years. His final bitterness and disillusion were vividly evidenced in the savagely satiric *Bouvard and Pécuchet,* left unfinished at his death in 1880.

Gustave Flaubert

THREE TALES

A Simple Heart

The Legend of St. Julian the Hospitaler

Herodias

A New Translation by Walter F. Cobb
With a Foreword by Henri Peyre

 A SIGNET CLASSIC

Published by THE NEW AMERICAN LIBRARY

COPYRIGHT © 1964 BY WALTER J. COBB
FOREWORD COPYRIGHT © 1964 BY
THE NEW AMERICAN LIBRARY OF WORLD LITERATURE, INC.

First Printing, January, 1964

SIGNET CLASSICS are published by
The New American Library of World Literature, Inc.
501 Madison Avenue, New York 22, New York

PRINTED IN THE UNITED STATES OF AMERICA

Contents

Foreword

Of all the works that Gustave Flaubert left behind him, none received such enthusiastic acclaim from his contemporaries as *Trois Contes;* none, not even *Madame Bovary,* so easily won the title of a classic and has been equally admired by the French pupil bent on training his style, by the student of French and of European fiction in many a land, and by the general public weary of the effete banality of many short stories intended for mass consumption in popular magazines. Not only do these tales constitute the fittest initiation to the rest of Flaubert's works, but they eschew the continuous tension, at times resulting in monotony, that may irk some readers of the longer novels, where nothing is ever left to chance and where too equal a light seems to suffuse all the episodes and all the characters.

Of Flaubert's rank among the eminent fiction writers of the great century of fiction there can be little debate. His detractors have arisen only in his own country: Marcel Proust found his style lacking in evocative power and in vivid imagery; Paul Valéry derided his arduous labor over his style, while he himself admired Mallarmé's ever more relentless quest for perfection and devoted months and years to the polishing of one poem; Jean-Paul Sartre indicted Flaubert for having preferred his cult of art to any Existentialist commitment to the "here and now." Outside France, dissent is almost unknown. Henry James was among the first to bestow on Flaubert the title of "a classic." Allen Tate credited him with truly having created modern fiction. In England, Osbert Sitwell confessed that never perhaps could his own country "hope to bring forth a novelist of such imaginative perfection, so polished and at the same time so full of fire, as Flaubert." Ernest Hemingway used to pay tribute to the bust of Flaubert in the Luxembourg gardens as to "one whom we loved unstintingly." Franz Kafka and James Joyce, the two most influential writers of contemporary European fiction, both bowed before the artistic economy, the mastery of precise language, the cumulative effects of the narrative, and the poetry blended with an almost scientific rigor that they descried in Flaubert's prose. To the varied merits that had slowly won acclaim for *Madame Bovary* (1857) and for *L'Éducation Sentimentale* (1869), Flaubert added, as he grew older, a warmer sense of compassion for human sorrows, so moving in the first of the *Three Tales;* a tragic anguish in the face of the fatality that drove Saint Julian to his doom and mankind in general to fits of destructive fury succeeded by repentance; a keener awareness of the role of ambition, fanaticism, cowardice, and lust in the rulers of nations, which is exemplified in "Herodias." Biographers and critics have generally hailed those three tales, Flaubert's last complete work, not only as his testament, but as the culmination and the summation of his literary career. "A Simple Heart" is laid in a modern setting in Flaubert's own province, like *Madame Bovary,* and represents a return to realism tempered with kindness. "Saint Julian" is a plunge into the past and the supernatural and gives free rein to the author's lifelong romantic nostalgia. "Herodias," like *Salammbô* (1862), conjures up the ancient world with its conflict of races and of faiths and voices Flaubert's fascination with the Orient.

Flaubert, born in 1821, was fifty-five when he published his *Three Tales* (1877), three years before he died. His nature was uncommonly sensitive and vulnerable. He, who was charged by contemporary critics with immorality and with offering "a heap of manure" to the public, was in fact an idealist and a dreamer. He was devoted to his family and deeply attached to his mother, extraordinarily loyal to his friends, easily wounded by the lack of comprehension in critics. The self-complacent callousness of the middle class, its mercantile greed, its acceptance of prosaic banality irked him. Like Cervantes and Molière before him, he resorted to satire and to irony in order to amend others and, perhaps, himself (for he, too, was an incurable bourgeois); he laughed at mankind's foibles instead of indulging in self-pity. He never married, and his solitary devotion to his art, his mad pursuit of cadences in his sentences, and his perspicuous use of exact language wearied him. He had suffered, at twenty-three, the first attack of a nervous disease that must have left him with a harrowing, lurking fear.

After 1871 a succession of griefs filled Flaubert with growing sadness. The defeat of France in the Franco-Prussian war, the invasion of his Normandy home by the Germans, the fury of the civil war in Paris during the Commune afflicted him deeply; for he never achieved the impassibility of which the advocates of art for art's sake dreamed. His mother died in 1872, three years after Flaubert's closest friend, Louis Bouilhet, had been carried away. Sainte-Beuve, Théophile Gautier, Michelet, whom he admired, also disappeared between 1869 and 1874. In 1876 it was to be the turn of Louise Colet, whom Flaubert had once ardently loved and taken as his literary confidante, and of George Sand, whom he revered. The husband of his niece suffered serious financial reverses and Flaubert, once free from financial worries, generously offered all he had to save him from bankruptcy. The last novel on which he was working, *Bouvard et Pécuchet,* a comic and yet a useful epic of human foolishness, was not going well and was to be left interrupted and inconclusive at Flaubert's sudden death. The melancholy of his moods is reflected in "A Simple Heart," which Flaubert composed as a last tribute to his native province and to the memories of his youth. A writer, he often contended, should no more intervene in his work than God does in nature; his duty was not to intrude with his subjective ego, his moralizing reflections, or with any falsification of the truth that is often bitter or tragic. But a personal experience lay at the source of much of what Flaubert wrote. He had observed in his own family middle-class women like Mme. Aubain, children brought up like Paul and Virginie, devoted and patient servants as attached to their masters as simplehearted Félicité. He had relatives at Pont-l'Évêque, knew every feature of the countryside, and, as a teen-ager, he had spent summers at Trouville. Indeed, his most tender memory, which he cherished to his dying day, was that of a lady whom he had seen on that beach (then far from fashionable and primitive in its facilities) and who had smiled to him when he had picked up her scarf, which the wind had blown away.

Flaubert spurned the label of "realist." To him and to many of his contemporaries, realism in literature implied brutality and squalor, the refusal to select and to organize, and stories or plays that were crude slices of life with no composition, no ultimate significance, none of the essential art of omission that great classics had always practiced. Fastidious selectiveness is the first virtue that impresses the reader as he opens the first of these stories. Time is suggested ("half a century" of loyal service), the envy of provincial women ever prone to spying on their neighbors, the irony of so much unrewarded devotion underlined by the name of "Félicité," which she bore. The second paragraph is made up of an enumeration of seven verbs, five in the imperfect, the tense through which Flaubert loved to convey the slow erosion of time; it already hints at the crabbed temper of her harsh mistress.

Then the circumstances are mentioned; one of the features of the story lies in its suggestion of a slow-moving, eventless existence in a corner of France apparently unmindful of Napoleonic wars, of foreign occupation, riots, revolutions, and economic crises. Neither politics nor religious controversies affect the laborious lives of the common people; the immorality credited to Paris never reached those austere devotees of their daily duty. The house, its furniture, its decoration, even its smells are then conjured up in a few sentences by the author, who never indulges in the saturation of which Balzac was fond in his descriptions. And the clean, thrifty, submissive servant is portrayed, with her features like those of a wooden statue.

The five sections of "A Simple Heart" are likewise made up of brief, concise paragraphs, from which any unessential detail has been banished. Section 2 enables us to catch a glimpse of Félicité's youth; for that ageless woman once was young and courted . . . and jilted. Five lines are enough for the author to depict her grief. She soon learned resignation and transferred all her capacity for affection to the two children of her employer, then to a nephew of hers, Victor, whom she chances to meet. That nephew, a sailor boy, dies of yellow fever in Havana; Virginie perishes from a lung disease; Paul, spoiled by his mother and by Félicité, turns out to be a good-for-nothing, as his father had been before him. The final sections of the tale are focused on the aging Félicité. All her tenderness and her uninformed piety, which was always puzzled by the picture of the Holy Ghost in the church, turn to a parrot she had been given: the bird reminded her of the exotic lands where her nephew had perished. But the parrot dies during a rigorous winter; Mme. Aubain precedes her servant to the grave. The closing pages depict Félicité, mistaking her stuffed parrot for the Holy Ghost, passing away, wizened and feeble-minded, on the day of the feast of Corpus Christi.

Flaubert refrains from commenting or from concluding. To conclude, he used to say, is foolish for an artist. Humble Félicité belonged to the poor in spirit and to the oppressed who do not even dream of revolting. Resignation and sacrifice made up her existence. The tale is sad and its general color is gray, unlike colorful "Herodias." But it is profoundly true and compelling. To his old friend George Sand, who upbraided him gently for being too harsh, Flaubert replied: "I work in the sincerity of my heart . . . I do not heap up desolation for the fun of it. I simply cannot alter my eyes." The milk of kindness and of compassion flows through those pages of subtle, but far from inhuman, artistry.

The story of Saint Julian, which was written first, in 1875—1876, has always been the most admired of the three tales by English-speaking readers, James Joyce among them. Its visionary quality. The swift and colorful vividness of its dream imagery are well calculated to delight the imagination of those who have, from their childhood on, been familiar with *Macbeth* and with *The Ancient Mariner*. Like Coleridge's verse tale, it demands a momentary suspension of disbelief. The legend of that ferocious hunter, avid for slaughter, who murdered his father and mother as it had been predicted to him he would, then lives in repentance and poverty and is carried to heaven by a leper whom he had assisted, was current in Spain, Italy, and France during the Middle Ages. It has been studied in a monograph by A.M. Gossez, *La Légende de Saint Julien l'Hospitalier* (Lille, 1903) and by Gédéon Huet in the *Mercure de France* of July 1, 1913. Flaubert may have known the celebrated Golden Legend, which related the lives of saints for the medieval minds. But his inspiration came, as he said, from a stained-glass window of the Rouen cathedral, in the northern aisle, facing the fourth arcade of the choir.

Flaubert recaptures with surprising deftness the atmosphere of the Middle Ages. The castle is described with exquisite justness in the choice of details; there Julian is born, and there a double prophecy hints to each of his parents what tragic fate will be his. Fatality pursues the young lord. He begins by killing a mouse, then birds, a pigeon, beasts in the forest, herds of stag. One day, at dusk, he mistakes the bonnet of his own mother for a stork and almost pierces her with his arrow. Aghast at his own avidity for slaughter, he flees his home and fights afar, gloriously.

His courage and his skill soon make him the leader of adventurers across Europe and Africa. He marries the daughter of an emperor whose throne he has saved. But the greed of hunting seizes him anew. After a scene of unequaled splendor, during which Julian is surrounded, as in a nightmare, with innumerable animals that seem to sneer at him, he returns home weary. His parents, having long wandered as pilgrims in search of their son, have just reached the castle where he lives with the Princess, his wife. She has, to honor her husband's parents, put them to sleep in her own bed. Julian, coming home in the dark and finding a bearded man in his wife's bed, massacres his father and mother. Remorse, atonement for his monstrous crime, humility of heart then make a saint of him. Again, the tale is one of sacrifice and martyrdom.

Never was Flaubert's prose more colorful and evocative, more sparing of all unessentials, and more enthralling than in this supernatural tale. It unrolls like a film or like a vivid dream, with the wealth of precise details that all lovers of language will cherish. Behind the naïveté of the legend, however, and the wealth of incidents, a graver meaning is implied. Like Oedipus or Othello, Julian suffered from a tragic flaw, a greed for power and a thirst for destruction symbolic of mankind. Through his strange thirst for blood and an almost Freudian death-drive alone could he reach humility, and through suffering inflicted on others and on himself he rose to saintliness.

On the same cathedral in Flaubert's native city of Rouen, on the northern tympanum, a beautiful work of sculpture represents the decapitation of Saint John the Baptist, with Salome dancing on her hands while the executioner brandishes his knife, ready for the sacrifice. Flaubert's imagination was fired by those images of Eastern treachery and cruelty and by the ferocious sensuality of the Orient. He had fed on such visions when he had traveled in Egypt, Syria, and Greece in his youth. Like Bonaparte, Chateaubriand, and later Barrès or Malraux, he was haunted by Asia. Archaeology and erudition may prove perilous to a novelist and exaggerate the esthetic distance between him and his readers, as Flaubert had experienced with his novel on Carthage, *Salammbô*. But, in 1876—1877, Flaubert, at the end of his career, felt he could give free rein to his passion for reliving the past and impregnating it with life. The praises of several of his friends, such as Hippolyte Taine, who preferred "Herodias" to his other tales, justified him.

Few are the readers today whose knowledge of Roman history and of the origins of Christianity is adequate to elucidate the allusions in the most learned and the most violent of the *Three Tales*. Flaubert drew much from Suetonius, the Latin historian who related the monstrous immorality of those Roman emperors like Tiberius and Caligula who, nevertheless, gave the ancient world its longest era of peace and prosperity. He also owes much to the Jewish historian Josephus, a Pharisee who organized the revolt of the Jews in the first century after Christ, was taken prisoner by the Romans, then liberated by Emperor Vespasian, whose name, Flavius, he adopted and added to his own out of gratitude.

The events so powerfully brought to life in the third of the *Three Tales* have haunted Western imagination for centuries. From Cranach, Ghirlandajo, and Rubens to the late nineteenth century, many are the painters who have been inspired by Salome's dance and the bloody head of the prophet presented on a tray to the Jewish king. Oscar Wilde wrote on the same theme a play in French, which inspired an opera by Richard Strauss. Flaubert was exceedingly careful to base every detail of his story on authentic archaeological or textual sources and yet not to stifle the reader's imaginative power with too much pedantry. He was convinced that history and fiction can work hand in hand. A minimum of clarification is not out of place for the common reader so that he may approach the tale without anything detracting from his enjoyment.

Herod Antipas, who trembled before the Roman governor Vitellius and the son of Vitellius, Aulus (the degenerate

minion of Emperor Tiberius, who stuffed himself with food
and, in the manner of decadent Romans, made himself
vomit in order to eat again), was the grandson of Herod
the Great ("Herod the King" of the gospel of Saint Matthew, under whose reign Jesus was born). His mother had
been one of Herod's eight wives. He was made Tetrarch
of Galilee by the will of his grandfather, confirmed in
that function by the Romans, and helped by Vitellius;
he was later deposed by the Romans and exiled in Gaul.
He died in A.D. 72. He repudiated his wife in order to
marry Herodias, herself a granddaughter of Herod the
Great by one of his successive wives. Herodias had first
married her own uncle, Herod-Philip, by whom she had
a daughter, Salome. She then left her husband to live at
the court of Herod Antipas, her first husband's brother;
she succeeded in bringing him to marry her, his niece.
The Jews were outraged at such immorality, and Saint
John the Baptist never ceased calling upon Herod to repu-
diate her and threatening them with divine wrath and the
people's ire.

Herodias could not by herself regain much influence over
her weak husband, fearful of antagonizing the mob and
the Romans; the latter knew that he had been ready to
betray them repeatedly. John the Baptist ("Iaokanann"),
whose raiment was of camel's hair and whose meat, says
Saint Matthew, was locusts and wild honey, wielded power
with the Jewish masses when, around the year A.D. 28,
he was bidding the people to repent, for the advent of the
Messiah had taken place and the kingdom of heaven was
at hand. Herod dallied out of cowardice, disturbed in the
midst of his dissolute life by twinges of conscience.

But Herodias held in reserve her daughter by her previous husband, young Salome. During the sumptuous feast
offered by Herod to the Romans and to his court, she had
the dancer appear. Flaubert displayed all the enticements
of his style in the description of the clothes and of the
body of the girl. In one of the exclamations of his earlier
Temptation of Saint Anthony, the novelist, long before
Freud, had written: "At every crossroad of the soul, O

Lust, your appeal is heard, and you appear at the end of every idea like the courtesan at the end of the streets." Salome whirled in her now languid, now vertiginous dance as if she mourned a god or died in his caressing arms. Herod, in a frenzied desire, promised her anything she wished. Instructed by her mother, she begged from her stepfather the head of Saint John the Baptist. Soon the head, held by the long hair, was placed by the executioner on a tray and presented to Salome. The Romans shrugged their shoulders, nonchalant and feeling superior to such foreign barbaric manners. The Jews took comfort in the thought that the Messiah would soon appear. The gospel of Saint Matthew, in which the scene is related in Chapter XIV, soberly says:

"And his head was brought in a charger, and given to the damsel; and she brought it to her mother.

"And his disciples came and took up the body, and buried it, and went and told Jesus."

The scene of the decapitation and of the erotic dance of Salome, coming after the splendid description of the landscape of Judea at the beginning of the tale and the elaborate visit of the Roman governor to the secret caves where Herod Antipas concealed his treasures, his weapons, his white horses, and his prisoner, ranks among the most haunting in French fiction. The style differs from the calculated parsimony of language that suited the more restrained story of *A Simple Heart*. It is rich and colorful, with exotic and sensuous touches dexterously placed here and there, yet never a note too much. Flaubert's romantic nature, which he strove all his life to curb, knew how to avoid garish rhetoric and the excesses of too unremitting a tension. Within thirty pages, the storyteller succeeded in encompassing the whole tragedy of fanaticism, lust, and cruelty in the ancient East and the confrontation between the Romans and the Jews in the first century of the Christian era. Rightly could the historian Taine congratulate Flaubert on his success in "Herodias" as the most difficult and the best of the *Three Tales,* conjuring up the conflict of races and the setting of early Christianity more vividly than any historian could ever do.

Henri Peyre
Yale University

A Simple Heart

❁ ❁ ❁

1

For half a century the womenfolk of Pont-l'Évêque begrudged Mme. Aubain her servant, Félicité.

For one hundred francs a year she cooked and did the housework, sewed, washed, ironed, and knew how to bridle a horse, how to "fatten" the chickens, how to make butter, and she remained loyal to her mistress who, it must be noted, was not a very easy person to get along with.

Mme. Aubain had married a handsome fellow, without means, who had died at the beginning of the year 1809, leaving her with two very young children and many debts. At that time she sold what landed property she possessed, except two farms, one at Toucques and another at Geffosses, the income of which brought her, at most, five thousand francs a year; and she gave up her house at Saint Melaine to move into another less costly to maintain—a house that had belonged to her ancestors and that was situated behind the market square.

This house, with its slate roof, stood between an alley and a little street that led to the river. Inside it had different levels which caused one to stumble. A narrow vestibule separated the kitchen from the parlor where Mme. Aubain, seated near the casement window in her wicker chair, spent the entire day. Against the wainscoting, painted white, were aligned eight mahogany chairs. A pyramid of wooden boxes and pasteboard cartons were piled up on an old piano, underneath a barometer. Two small stuffed armchairs flanked the yellow marble fireplace, in the style of Louis XV. The clock in the center depicted a temple of

Vesta—the whole room smelled slightly musty, because the floor was on a level lower than the garden.

On the first floor, there was first Madame's bedroom, very large, papered in a pale flower design, with a portrait of "Monsieur" in a foppish costume on the wall. A smaller room in which were to be seen two children's beds, without mattresses, adjoined hers. Next came the salon, always kept locked, and cluttered with furniture covered over with sheets. Then a corridor led to the study; books and miscellaneous papers filled the shelves of a bookcase, the three sections of which surrounded a large desk made of black wood. The two panels in the corner were almost completely covered with pen sketches, water colors, and engravings by Audran—souvenirs of better times and vanished luxury. A dormer window on the second floor lighted Félicité's room, which overlooked the fields.

Félicité rose at daybreak so as not to miss mass, and she worked till evening without interruption; then, when dinner was over, the dishes done, the door bolted, she would smother the burning log in the ashes and fall asleep before the hearth, her rosary beads still in her hand. No one was better at stubborn bargaining in the marketplace than she. As for cleanliness, the shine on her pots and pans was the despair of the other servants. Very thrifty, she ate slowly and gathered together with her finger the bread crumbs on the table—her bread, which weighed twelve pounds, was especially baked for her, and lasted twenty days.

During all seasons she wore a calico neckerchief over her shoulders, pinned at the back, a bonnet hiding her hair, gray stockings, a red petticoat, and over her bodice an apron like those worn by hospital nurses.

Her face was thin and her voice sharp. At twenty-five, people took her to be forty. After she reached fifty, she showed no age at all; and always taciturn, with her erect posture and measured movements, she seemed like a woman made of wood, performing like an automaton.

2

Like any other, Félicité had had her love story.

Her father, a stonemason, had been killed by a fall from a scaffold. Then her mother died, her sisters wandered away, a farmer took her in and employed her, while still very young, to watch over his cows in the pasture. She shivered in her thin rags; drank water, lying on her stomach, from ponds; for no reason received whippings, and finally was sent away because of a theft of thirty sous—a crime she had not committed. She went to another farm, tended the poultry yard, and because she pleased her employers the other servants became jealous of her.

One evening in August (she was then eighteen) she was taken to a party at Colleville. Immediately she was bewildered, dazzled by the noise of the fiddlers, the lights hanging from the trees, the medley of costumes, the laces, the gold crosses, the immense crowd of people all bustling about. She was standing modestly aside, when a young, well-dressed man, smoking a pipe while resting his elbows on the shaft of a cart, came over and asked her to dance. He bought her cider, coffee and cakes, and a silk scarf, and, imagining that she guessed what he was thinking about, offered to take her home. On their way past a field of oats, he threw her backward very roughly. She was frightened and began to scream. He ran off.

Another evening, on the road to Beaumont, she wanted to pass a large wagon of hay that was going along slowly, and brushing against the wheels, she recognized Théodore.

He addressed her calmly, saying that she must forgive him everything, since it was "the fault of the drink."

She did not know what to say; and she wanted to run away.

Immediately he began to speak about the harvesting and the important people of the commune, for his father had left Colleville and had taken over the farm at Écots, so that now they were neighbors. "Oh!" she said. He went on to say that they wanted him to settle down. However, he was in no hurry, and was going to wait till he found a wife to his taste. She lowered her head. Then he asked her had she thought of marriage. She replied, smiling, that it wasn't nice to make fun of her.

"But I'm not making fun of you, I swear!" said he, putting his left arm around her waist. She walked along leaning on him. They slowed their pace. The wind was gentle, stars were shining; in front of them the huge hay wagon swayed from side to side; the four horses, dragging their hoofs, were stirring up dust. Then suddenly the horses veered to the right. He kissed her once more. She disappeared into the darkness.

The following week, Théodore had several meetings with her.

They met in remote farmyards, behind walls, or under some isolated tree. She was not innocent like well-bred young ladies—she had learned from being around animals; but reason and her self-esteem kept her from giving in. Her resistance exasperated Théodore's passion, so much so that to satisfy it (or perhaps naïvely) he proposed marriage to her. At first she doubted his sincerity, but he made strong vows of love.

Soon afterward, he confessed to her a troublesome bit of news: his parents, the year before, had bought him a substitute for the army, but any day now he could be drafted again; the idea of military service frightened him. Félicité interpreted this cowardice as proof of his affection, and it redoubled hers. She stole away at night to meet him, and while they were together Théodore tortured her with his problems and entreaties.

At last, he declared that he would go himself to the prefecture for information, and that he would inform her of what he found out on the following Sunday, between eleven o'clock and midnight.

When the moment arrived she hastened to her lover.

In his stead, she found one of his friends.

He told her that she was never to see Théodore again. To prevent himself from being drafted, Théodore had married a very rich *old* lady, Mme. Lehoussais of Toucques.

Félicité, beside herself with grief, threw herself to the ground, uttering cries, and calling upon the merciful God above. All alone she stayed there in the fields, and wept till morning. Then she went back to the farm and announced that she was leaving; and, at the end of the month, when she had received her wages, she bundled up her few little belongings in a handkerchief and went to Pont-l'-Évêque.

In front of the inn, she made some inquiries of a woman wearing a widow's cap, and who, it just so happened, was looking for a cook. This young girl did not know much, but she seemed so willing and was asking for so little that Mme. Aubain ended by saying: "All right, I'll take you!"

Fifteen minutes later, Félicité was settled in her new house.

At first, she lived there in a sort of fear and trembling caused by "the tone of the house" and by the vivid memory of "Monsieur" which hovered over everything! Madame's children, Paul and Virginie, one seven and the other four, respectively, seemed to her to be made of some rare substance; she liked to carry them piggyback. But Mme. Aubain forbade her to kiss them too often, which mortified Félicité. However, she was happy. The gentleness of her surroundings had softened her grief.

Every Thursday, the close friends of Mme. Aubain used to come for a game of "Boston." Félicité had to get the cards and foot warmers ready in advance. They always arrived precisely at eight and left before the clock struck eleven.

Every Monday morning, the junk dealer who lived on

the same street used to spread out his wares on the ground. Then the whole town was filled with the hum of many voices—together with the neighing of horses, the bleating of sheep, the grunting of pigs, and the rattle of carts down the street. About noon, when market time reached its peak, a tall, old peasant with a hooked nose, wearing his cap on the back of his head, would appear and stand in the door-way—this was Robelin, a farmer of Geffosses. A little while later, Liébard, a farmer from Toucques, short, ruddy, corpulent, wearing a gray coat and spurs, appeared in the same place.

Both brought chickens and cheeses to their landlady, Mme. Aubain. Invariably Félicité would cunningly outwit them, and they would go away with more respect for her shrewdness.

At various times, the Marquis of Gremanville, one of Mme. Aubain's uncles, used to visit her. He had ruined himself by debauchery and was now living in Falaise on his last bit of farmland. He invariably came at lunch time, accompanied by a dreadful poodle that always dirtied the furniture with its paws. Despite his efforts to play the role of the gentleman (he would raise his hat every time he said, "my late father"), force of habit compelled him to drink one glass after another and to blurt out risqué stories. Félicité would politely usher him out the door, saying "You have had enough, Monsieur de Gremanville! Some other time!" And she would shut the door on him.

To M. Bourais, a retired lawyer, the door was invitingly opened. His white cravat, his bald head, his frilled shirt, his full-fitting brown frock coat, his way of flourishing his arm when he took snuff—his whole person produced in her a certain excitement such as we all experience at the sight of extraordinary men.

As he was the manager of Madame's properties, he spent hours with her in "Monsieur's" study, all the time fearful of compromising his position. He had great respect for the bench. Moreover, he had some pretensions to being a Latin scholar.

To make learning pleasant for the children, he gave

them a geography book consisting of prints. There were representative scenes from all over the world: cannibals with feathered headdresses; a monkey carrying away a damsel; Bedouins in the desert; a whale being harpooned, and so on.

Paul explained these pictures to Félicité. And this was the extent of her literary education.

The children's education was in the hands of Guyot, a wretched individual working at the Town Hall, who was famous for his beautiful handwriting and for the way he sharpened his penknife on his boot.

When the weather was clear, they all used to start early for the Geffosses farm.

The farmyard is on the side of a slope, with the house in the middle; and the sea, from a distance, looks like a gray blot.

Félicité would take out slices of cold meat from her basket, and they all would eat in a room that adjoined the milk house. It was all that remained of a once elegant country house. Now the wallpaper hung like tattered ribbons, and rustled with the drafts from the window. Mme. Aubain would bow her head, weighed down by memories of the past; the children would no longer dare to speak. "Go out and play!" she would say to them; and off they would go.

Paul climbed up in the barn, caught birds, played ducks and drakes, or tapped with a stick the huge barrels that rumbled like drums.

Virginie fed the rabbits and scampered away to pick cornflowers, her legs moving so quickly that you could see her little lace-trimmed drawers.

One autumn evening they were returning through the fields.

The moon in its first quarter lit a segment of the sky, and a haze floated like a scarf over the winding Toucques river. Cattle, lying in the middle of the meadow, gazed contentedly at these four people. In the third pasture, some of the cows got up and circled them. "Don't be afraid!" said Félicité, and stroking the back of the one nearest to her, she murmured a sort of lament. It turned around and the others did the same. But, when they crossed the next field, they heard a loud bellow. It was a bull, hidden in the haze. He came toward the two women. Mme. Aubain was about to run. "No, no, not so fast!" Nevertheless, though they quickened their steps, they heard back of them the sound of snorting, coming closer and closer. His hoofs beat like hammer blows on the meadow grass. Now he was galloping toward them! Félicité turned around and, with both hands, snatched up clods of turf to throw into the bull's eyes. He lowered his head, shook his horns, and, trembling with fury, bellowed terribly. Mme. Aubain, at the end of the pasture with the two little ones, looked frantically for a way to get over the high bank. Félicité backed steadily away from the bull, throwing grass and dirt at him all the time, to blind him, while at the same time she shouted, "Hurry! Hurry!"

Mme. Aubain jumped into the ditch, pushing Virginie, then Paul, in front of her. She stumbled several times, struggling to climb the bank, and by sheer courage finally succeeded.

The bull had backed Félicité against a fence; his slaver spattered her face; a second more and he would have gored her. She just had time to crawl between two fence rails. The huge animal stopped, amazed.

At Pont l'Évêque, they talked of this adventure for many years. However, Félicité was not proud of it, nor did she think that she had done anything heroic.

Virginie took up all her time—for, as a result of her fright, she had developed a nervous disorder, and M. Poupart, the physician, advised sea-baths for her at Trouville.

At that time not many people frequented Trouville. Mme. Aubain sought information about the place, consulted with Bourais, and made preparations as if embarking on a long voyage.

They sent off her baggage the day before, in Liébard's cart. The next day, he brought to the house two horses, one of which had a lady's saddle, with a velvet back;

the other had a cloak rolled up like a seat on the crupper.

Mme. Aubain mounted her horse, behind Liébard. Félicité took charge of Virginie, and Paul rode M. Lechaptois' donkey, lent to him on condition that he take good care of it.

The road was so bad that it took two hours to go five miles. The horses sank into mud up to their pasterns, and had to make strenuous movements with their haunches to extricate themselves; they would sometimes stumble in ruts; other times they had to leap over them. In some places Liébard's mare would stop all of a sudden. Patiently he would wait for her to go on again; meantime he talked about the people whose property bordered the road, interpolating moral reflections on the story told. Thus, while they were in the middle of Toucques, as they were passing under a window full of nasturtiums, he remarked, shrugging his shoulders: "There's that Mme. Lehoussais, who instead of taking in a young man . . ." Félicité did not hear the rest; the horses were trotting; the donkey was galloping. They all filed down the path, a gate swung open, two boys appeared, and they dismounted in front of a dung heap on the very threshold.

When Mme. Liébard spotted her mistress, she was profuse in her expressions of delight. She served her a luncheon of sirloin of beef, tripe, black pudding, a fricassee of chicken, frothy cider, a fruit tart, and plums in brandy—all the time paying the Madame polite compliments, saying how wonderful she looked, how Mademoiselle was becoming "magnificent," and how Paul was growing so strong. Nor did she forget their deceased grandparents, whom the Liébards had known, as they had been in the service of the family for generations. The farm, like them, had the quality of oldness. The ceiling beams were worm-eaten, the walls black with smoke, the window panes gray with dust. On an oak sideboard were set all sorts of utensils, jugs, dishes, pewter bowls, wolf-traps, and sheep shears; and a big syringe made the children laugh. There was not a tree in the three courtyards that did not have mushrooms growing at its base or a tuft of mistletoe on its branches.

The wind had blown some of the trees down. They had begun to grow again in the middle; and all of them were bent under the weight of the apples. The thatched roofs, like brown velvet and varying in thickness, had withstood the most violent gales. However, the wagon shed was falling into ruin. Mme. Aubain said she would tend to it later, and ordered the animals to be resaddled.

It was another half hour before they arrived in Trouville. The little caravan dismounted to pass Écores—a cliff jutting out over some boats—and three minutes later, at the end of the quay, they entered the courtyard of the "Golden Lamb" kept by Mme. David.

Virginie, from the very first days there, began to feel less weak—the result of the change of air and the effect of the baths, which she took in her chemise, for want of a bathing costume. Her nurse dressed her in a custom-house shed, which was used by the bathers.

In the afternoon, with the donkey, they rode off beyond the Roches-Noires, in the direction of Hennequeville. The path rose, at first, over hilly terrain like the lawn of a park; then it reached a plateau where meadows alternated with plowed fields. By the edge of the road, in briar thickets, stood holly bushes; here and there, a great lifeless tree made zigzags in the blue sky with its naked branches.

Nearly always they would rest awhile in a meadow, with Deauville to their left, Le Havre to the right, and before them the open sea. It sparkled in the sun, smooth like a mirror, so calm that you could hardly hear its murmuring. Unseen sparrows chirped, and the immense vault of heaven hung over everything. Mme. Aubain sat on the ground, doing her sewing; Virginie, next to her, plaited rushes; Félicité was weeding some lavender flowers; Paul was bored and wanted to go back.

On other occasions, they would go by boat across the Toucques, looking for shells. At low tide, they found sea urchins, starfish, and jellyfish; and the children would chase the flakes of foam carried by the wind. The waves, breaking on the sand, unrolled sleepily along the beach. The latter stretched as far as you could see, but on the landward side, it ended in the dunes that separated it from the Marais, a wide meadow shaped like an arena. When they returned that way, Trouville, on the hill slope in the background, loomed larger with every step, and its houses, with their uneven rooftops, seemed to be spread in colorful disorder.

On days when it was too hot, they did not leave their room. The dazzling brightness from outside made golden streaks through the venetian blinds. The village was silent. No one was to be seen on the sidewalks below. The all-pervading silence intensified the peacefulness. In the distance the hammers of the caulkers tapped on the hulls of the boats and a warm breeze wafted up the odor of tar.

The chief amusement was watching the ships return. As soon as they has passed the buoys, they began to maneuver. They lowered the sails on two of the three masts, and, with the foresail swelling like a balloon, they moved in gliding fashion over the chopping waves, until they reached the middle of the harbor where they suddenly dropped anchor. Then the boat docked against the pier. The sailors threw squirming fish over the side; a line of carts was awaiting them, and women in cotton bonnets rushed forward to take the baskets and to kiss their men.

One day one of them came up to Félicité, who, a little later, went to her room overjoyed. She had found a sister, Nastasie Barette, whose married name was Leroux, nursing an infant; and on her right-hand side was another child, and at her left was a little cabin boy with his hands on his hips and a beret cocked over his ear.

After fifteen minutes, Mme. Aubain sent them away.

But they were always to be seen outside her kitchen or on their walks. The husband never appeared.

Félicité took a liking to them. She bought them a blanket, some shirts, and a stove; it was obvious they were taking advantage of her. And this weakness of hers annoyed Mme. Aubain, who, moreover, did not like the familiar ways of Félicité's nephew with her son. And, as Virginie was coughing and the weather was no longer good, she decided to go back to Pont-l'Évêque.

M. Bourais advised her on the choice of a school for

Paul. The one at Caen was considered to be the best, so he was sent there. He said his goodbyes bravely and was content to be going to live in a house where he would have companions his age.

Mme. Aubain resigned herself to her son's departure, because it was necessary. Virginie thought about it less and less. Félicité missed his noise. But a new interest diverted her: from Christmas time onward, she took the little girl to her catechism lesson every day.

3

When she had made her genuflection at the door of the church, Félicité walked under the lofty nave between the double row of chairs, opened Mme. Aubain's pew, sat down, and gazed around.

The choir stalls were filled with boys on the right and girls on the left; the curé was standing next to the lectern. One stained-glass window in the apse depicted the Holy Ghost hovering over the Virgin; another showed her on her knees before the Christ Child, and behind the tabernacle a group carved in wood depicted St. Michael overcoming the dragon.

The priest began with an outline of Sacred History. Félicité formed vivid pictures in her mind of Paradise, the Flood, the Tower of Babel, cities in flames, people dying, idols being overturned. She learned from these bewildering scenes a reverence for the Most High and a fear of His wrath. Then, she wept when the Passion was narrated. Why had they crucified Him—He who loved the little children, He who fed the multitudes, He who cured the blind, and He who had consented, out of meekness, to be born among the poor in a stable? The sowings, the harvests, the wine presses, all these familiar things the Gospel speaks of, were a part of her life; they had been sanctified by God's sojourn on earth. She loved lambs more tenderly out of love for the Lamb, and doves because of the Holy Ghost.

She found it difficult to imagine His person, for He was not only a bird, but a flame as well, and at still other times, a breath. She thought perhaps it is His light that hovers at night on the edge of the marshes, His breath that moves the clouds, His voice that gives the bells their harmony! Thus she sat in adoration, delighting in the cool walls and the peacefulness of the church.

As for Church dogmas, she did not understand or even try to understand them. The priest gave his sermon, the children recited, and she finally fell asleep. She woke up again with a start, when the people, leaving the church, clattered with their wooden shoes on the flagstones.

This is how Félicité, whose religious education had been neglected in her youth, learned her catechism—by hearing it repeated; and from that time on she imitated all of Virginie's practices, fasting when she did and going to confession with her. On Corpus Christi they made a small altar together.

She had looked forward with consternation to Virginie's first communion. Félicité made much ado about the little girl's rosary beads, her shoes, her prayerbook, her gloves. How she trembled as she helped Virginie's mother dress the child!

All through the mass, Félicité felt a terrible anxiety. She could not see one side of the choir—M. Bourais was in the way; but just in front of her, the band of young virgins, wearing white crowns over their lowered veils, looked to her like a field of snow. From afar she could recognize her precious little Virginie by her slender neck and by her enraptured bearing.

The altar bell tinkled. Heads bowed. There was silence. When the organ began to play again, the choir members and the whole congregation chanted the *Agnus Dei*. Then the boys began to move from their pews. After them the girls rose. Reverently, with their hands joined, they made their way to the brilliantly lit altar, and knelt on the first step, to receive the Divine Host in turn. Afterward they came back to their *prie-dieus* in the same order.

When it was Virginie's turn, Félicité leaned forward to see her; and in imagination, stimulated by genuine affection, she felt that she herself was this child. Virginie's face became her own; Virginie's dress clothed her; Virginie's heart throbbed in her own breast; when Virginie opened her mouth and closed her eyes, Félicité almost fainted.

Early the next morning, she went to the sacristy and asked M. le Curé to give her communion. She received it with devotion, but she did not feel the same ecstatic rapture.

Mme. Aubain wanted to make an accomplished person of her daughter; and, as Guyot could not teach her either English or music, she decided to board Virginie in the Ursuline Convent at Honfleur.

Virginie did not object. Félicité sighed and thought Madame was unfeeling. Then she decided that her mistress was, perhaps, right. These things were too much for Félicité to grasp.

So, one day, an old coach stopped in front of the door, and out stepped a nun who had come to fetch Virginie. Félicité lifted Virginie's baggage to the top of the vehicle, gave some instructions to the driver, and put on the seat six jars of jam, a dozen pears, and a bouquet of violets.

Virginie, at the last moment, began to sob; she hugged her mother who kissed her on the forehead and kept saying, "Come on, now! Be brave. Don't cry!" The side step was raised and the coach drove off.

Then Mme. Aubain broke down. That evening all her friends—the Lormeau family, Mme. Lechaptois, the Rochefeville ladies, M. de Houppeville, and Bourais—came to comfort her.

At first, her daughter's absence caused Mme. Aubain much grief. But three times a week she received a letter from Virginie. She wrote to her daughter on the other days, took strolls in the garden, or read a little, and in this way managed to fill the lonely hours.

Every morning, regularly, Félicité would go into Virginie's room and look around. It distressed her not to have to comb the girl's hair any more, not to lace her shoes, not to tuck her into bed—not to see her perpetually radiant face, not to hold her hand anymore when they went out together. For want of something to do, Félicité tried making lace, but her clumsy fingers broke the threads; she could not do anything, she could not sleep, and was, to use her own expression, "done in." To "distract herself," she asked permission to have her nephew Victor visit her.

He came on Sundays after mass—rosy-cheeked, bare-chested, and smelling of the fields he had crossed. Immediately Félicité set the table and they sat down to lunch facing each other. Félicité, eating as little as possible to save expense, stuffed him so much that finally he fell asleep. When vespers sounded, she woke him, brushed his trousers, knotted his tie, and went to the church with him, leaning on his arm with a kind of maternal pride.

His parents always instructed him to get something out of her—either a box of brown sugar, some soap, some brandy, or sometimes even money. He always brought his old clothes to Félicité to be mended. She was happy to do this task because it meant he had to come back.

In August his father took him off on a cruise along the coast.

It was vacation time, and the arrival of the children consoled her in the absence of her nephew. But Paul was getting contrary and Virginie was now too old to be addressed familiarly. Now there was a barrier—a feeling of uneasiness—between Virginie and Félicité.

Victor went to Morlaix, Dunkirk, and then to Brighton; and on his return from each trip he brought Félicité a present. The first time it was a box made of sea shells; then it was a coffee cup; from his third trip it was a large gingerbread man. Victor was becoming good-looking: he was well-built, he wore a small mustache, his eyes were attractively frank, and he cocked his small leather cap back like a pilot's. He amused her by telling stories mixed with sailors' lingo.

One Monday, July 14, 1819 (she never forgot the date), Victor told her that he had signed up for a long voyage, and that during the night of the following day, he would take the Honfleur boat to join his schooner which was to weigh anchor from Le Havre soon afterward. He would, perhaps, be gone for two years.

The thought of such a long absence dismayed Félicité, and, to say goodbye to him again, on Wednesday evening, after Madame's dinner, she put on her clogs and traveled the long twelve miles between Pont-l'Évêque and Honfleur.

When she arrived at the Calvary instead of turning left, she went right, got lost in the shipyards, and had to retrace her steps. Some people whom she approached advised her to hurry along. She went all around the ship-filled harbor, stumbling over the moorings. Where the ground sloped, lights criss-crossed. Félicité thought she was losing her mind, for she saw horses in the heavens.

On the wharf's edge, horses, frightened by the sea, were neighing. A crane was lifting them and lowering them into a boat where passengers were jostling one another amid cider casks, baskets of cheese, and grain sacks. Over the cackling of the chickens, one could hear the captain cursing. A cabin boy, undisturbed by all the confusion, leaned over the bow.

Félicité, who had not recognized him, suddenly called, "Victor!" He raised his head; she darted toward him, but at that moment the gangplank was raised.

The boat, towed by singing women, eased away from the wharf. Her hull creaked, and heavy water lashed against the prow. The sail had been turned around, hence no one could be seen any longer on her decks. On the silvery, moonlit sea, she became a black spot that gradually faded out of sight, then sank below the horizon.

As Félicité passed Calvary she wanted to commend to God this boy whom she loved most. She stood there a long time praying, her face bathed in tears, her eyes raised to heaven.

The town slept; only custom officials walked about. There was the sound of water, like that of a torrent, pouring through the holes of a sluice. The town clock struck two.

The convent reception room would not be open before morning. If she was late, Madame would surely be annoyed; so, in spite of a great desire to see Virginie, she returned home. The serving girls of the inn were just getting up when she reached Pont-l'Évêque.

"For months and months that poor boy is going to be tossing about on the waves!" thought Félicité. She had not been frightened by his previous voyages. One always returned safely from England or Brittany; but America, the colonies, the islands—all these were lost in a hazy region at the other end of the world.

From this moment on, Félicité thought of nothing but her nephew. On sunny days, she imagined he was thirsty; when it was stormy, she feared for him the lightning. As she listened to the wind howling down the chimney or heard it carrying off the slates, she saw him battered by this same storm, as he clung to the top of a broken masthead, his body bent back under the wash of the waves. At other times—remembering the geography prints —she imagined him being eaten by cannibals, captured by apes in the jungle, or lying dead on some deserted beach. But never did she speak of these secret apprehensions.

Mme. Aubain had her own apprehensions about her daughter.

The good nuns thought Virginie an affectionate but delicate child. The least bit of excitement upset her. She had to give up her piano lessons.

Her mother demanded from the convent authorities a regular flow of letters. One morning when there was no mail, she became very impatient; she walked up and down her room from the chair to the window. It was very strange indeed! No mail in four days!

To console her, Félicité said, "Look at me, Madame, it has been six months since I received any . . . !"

"From whom? . . ."

"Why . . . from my nephew!" meekly replied the servant.

"Oh! your nephew!" Mme. Aubain began to pace again, shrugging her shoulders as if to say: "I wasn't thinking of him! . . . Besides, he is nothing to me! A cabin boy, a little scamp! . . . While my daughter . . . just think!"

Félicité, though accustomed to rudeness, felt indignant at Madame, but overlooked it as usual.

It seemed very natural to her that one could lose one's head over a little girl.

The two children, Virginie and her nephew, were equally dear to her—they both shared her heart! And their destinies were to be the same.

The druggist told her that Victor's boat had docked in Havana. He had read this bit of news in a newspaper.

On account of cigars, she imagined Havana to be a country where everyone did nothing but smoke. She could visualize Victor moving among the Negroes in a cloud of tobacco fumes. Could one "in case of necessity" return from Havana by land, she wondered. How far was it from Pont-l'Évêque? For answers to these questions, she turned to M. Bourais.

He took out his atlas and began explaining longitudes; and smiled in a pedantic manner at Félicité's amazement. Then with his pencil he pointed to an almost imperceptible black dot on an oval spot, and said, "Here it is." She leaned over the map. This network of colored lines blurred her vision and meant nothing to her; and when Bourais asked her to say what was puzzling her, she begged him to point to the house where Victor was staying. Bourais threw up his arms, sneezed, and roared with laughter; such simplicity was sheer joy to him. But Félicité did not understand why he was so amused—how could she when she perhaps expected to see her nephew's portrait on the map—so limited was her understanding!

It was two weeks afterward that Liébard came into the kitchen at market time as usual, and handed her a letter from her brother-in-law. Since neither of them could read, she took it to her mistress.

Mme. Aubain, who was counting stitches in her knitting, put her work aside, opened the letter, trembled, and with a look full of meaning, said in a low voice, "It is bad news . . . that they have to tell you. Your nephew . . . ."

He was dead. The letter said no more.

Félicité slumped into a chair, and leaned her head back.

She closed her eyelids which had suddenly become pink. Then, with her head down, her hands hanging idly, her eyes fixed, she kept saying over and over, "Poor boy! Poor little boy!"

Liébard, murmuring sighs of consolation, watched her. Mme. Aubain was still shaking a little. She suggested to Félicité that she go visit with her sister at Trouville.

Félicité made a gesture to indicate there was no need to do so.

There was silence. Liébard thought it wise that they leave Félicité alone.

Then Félicité said, "They don't care! It means nothing to them!"

She dropped her head again, but, from time to time, she mechanically picked up the long knitting needles from the worktable.

Women passed in the courtyard with their barrows of dripping linen.

Seeing them through the window, Félicité remembered her own washing. Having soaked it the day before, she had to rinse it today; and she left the room.

Her plank and wooden bucket were down by the Toucques. She threw a pile of underclothing on the river bank, rolled up her sleeves, and took the paddle in her hand. The heavy beating she gave her laundry could be heard in the nearby gardens. The meadows were empty, the wind made ripples on the surface of the water; while deep down, tall weeds swayed, like the hair of corpses floating in the water. Félicité suppressed her grief and was very brave till evening; but in her room, she broke down completely and lay on her bed with her face buried in the pillow and her hands clenched against her temples.

Much later, she heard from the captain himself the circumstances of Victor's death. He had had yellow fever. Four doctors had held him while they bled him—too much—at the hospital. He died immediately and the head doctor said: "There! Another one!"

Victor's parents had always been brutal to him. Félicité preferred not to see them again; and they in turn made no attempt to see her, either because they had forgotten about her, or because of the callousness of the poor.

Meanwhile, at the convent, Virginie became weaker. Congestion in her lungs, coughing, a continuous fever, and splotches on her cheekbones indicated some deep-seated illness. M. Poupart prescribed a few days in Provence. Mme. Aubain agreed to that, and would have brought her daughter home at once were it not for the climate of Pont-l'Évêque.

She chartered a carriage and was driven to the convent every Tuesday. There is a terrace in the garden from which you can see the Seine. Virginie would walk there on her mother's arm, over the fallen vine leaves. Sometimes the sun piercing through the clouds made her blink, as she gazed at the distant sails and the whole horizon— from the Château of Tancarville to the lighthouse of Le Havre. Then they would rest under an arbor. Her mother had with her a little flask of excellent Malaga wine, and, laughing at the idea of getting a little tipsy, Virginie would drink just a little, no more.

She regained strength. Autumn passed pleasantly. Félicité reassured Mme. Aubain. But, one evening when she had been running errands in the neighborhood, she saw on her return M. Poupart's carriage in front of the door. He was in the vestibule. Mme. Aubain was tying on her hat.

"Give me my foot warmer, my handbag, and gloves! Hurry!"

Virginie had pneumonia. Perhaps her case was already hopeless.

"Not yet!" said the doctor and both got into his carriage, under whirling flakes of snow. Night was falling. It was very cold.

Félicité rushed into church to light a candle. Then she ran after the carriage which she overtook an hour later. She had jumped nimbly on behind, and was holding on to the straps, when she suddenly thought: "The courtyard isn't locked! Suppose thieves break in!" And she jumped off.

At dawn of the following day, she went to the doctor's house. He had returned, but had left again for the country. Then she stayed at the inn, thinking some stranger would bring a letter. Finally, at dusk, she took the Lisieux stage-coach.

The convent was at the bottom of a steep lane. About half way down, Félicité heard strange sounds—a death knell. "It's for someone else," she thought. But she knocked violently on the door.

After several minutes, she heard the shuffling of slip-pers; the door was opened a crack and a nun appeared.

The good sister, with a compassionate air, said that Virginie "had just passed away." At that moment, the tolling at Saint-Léonard's became louder.

Félicité went up to the second floor of the convent.

From the doorway she could see Virginie lying on her back, her hands folded, her mouth open, and her head tilted back under an overhanging black cross between two motionless curtains, less pale than her face. Mme. Aubain, clutching the foot of the bed, was sobbing uncontrollably. The Mother Superior was standing on the right. Three candles on the dresser made shafts of red light, and mist whitened the windowpanes. Some nuns led Mme. Aubain away.

For two nights Félicité did not leave her death watch. She repeated the same prayers, sprinkled the sheets with holy water, sat down again, and gazed at the dead girl. At the end of the first night, she noticed that the face had yellowed, the lips had turned blue, the nose was sharper and the eyes were deeper. She kissed them several times, and would not have been surprised if they had opened again; for to minds like hers the supernatural is quite simple. She dressed her, wrapped her in a shroud, laid her body in the coffin, arranged her hair and placed a wreath upon her head. The hair was blond and extraor-dinarily long for her age. Félicité cut a thick lock of it and slipped half of it into Virginie's bosom. She resolved never to part with hers.

The corpse was brought back to Pont-l'Évêque, according to the wishes of Mme. Aubain, who followed the hearse in a closed carriage.

After the mass, it took another three-quarters of an hour to reach the cemetery. Paul, sobbing, walked ahead of the cortege. M. Bourais walked behind, followed by the principal residents of the village, the women wearing black mantles, and Félicité. She was thinking of her nephew, and because she had not been able to pay these respects to him, her sadness was intensified, as if he were being interred with Virginie.

Mme. Aubain's despair knew no limits.

At first she cried out against God, thinking it unjust for Him to have taken her daughter—Virginie who had never hurt anyone, and whose soul was so pure! But no! She should have taken her to the south. Other doctors could have saved her! She railed at herself, she wanted to join Virginie in death, she cried out distressfully in her dreams. One dream especially haunted her. Her husband, dressed like a sailor, came back from a long voyage and told her tearfully that he had received orders to take Virginie away. Then, they both tried to find a hiding place somewhere.

Once Mme. Aubain came in from the garden terribly upset. A little while before (she could point out the spot) the father and daughter, standing side by side, had appeared to her; they did nothing; they just looked at her.

For several months she kept to her room—apathetic. Félicité reproached her gently, saying her mistress must take care of herself for the sake of her son, and in remembrance of "her."

"Her?" replied Mme. Aubain as though she were emerging from sleep. "Ah yes! . . . Yes! You do not forget her!" This was an allusion to the cemetery which Mme. Aubain was strictly forbidden to visit.

Félicité went there every day.

At exactly four o'clock, she would go by the houses, climb the hill, open the gate, and come to Virginie's grave. There was a little column of pink marble with a plaque at its base, to which was fastened a chain that enclosed a miniature garden. The borders disappeared under beds of flowers. Félicité watered the plants, upturned the gravel, and knelt down better to dress the ground. Mme. Aubain, when at last she could visit the grave, felt a relief and a kind of consolation.

The years slipped by uneventfully and without any incidents other than the return of the great feast days: Easter, Assumption, All Saints' Day. Only household events were spoken of as important in the years that followed: for example, in 1825, two workmen whitewashed the vestibule; in 1827, part of the roof, falling into the courtyard, almost killed a man; in the summer of 1827, it became Madame's turn to offer the consecrated bread; Bourais, about this time, was mysteriously not around; and the old acquaintances one by one went away: Guyot, Liébard, Mme. Lechaptois, Robelin, Uncle Gremanville, who had been paralyzed for a long time now.

One night the driver of the mail coach announced in Pont-l'Évêque the July Revolution. A new subprefect was appointed a few days later: Baron de Larsonnière, an ex-consular official in America, and a man who had brought with him, in addition to his wife, his sister-in-law and her three daughters, almost grown up. They could be seen on their lawn, dressed in loose-fitting blouses; they had a Negro servant and a parrot. They paid a visit to Mme. Aubain, who returned their call promptly. Whenever Félicité saw them coming, she always ran to her mistress to forewarn her. But the only thing really capable of arousing Madame was letters from her son.

He could not follow any profession, since he spent most of his time in taverns. She paid his debts, but he contracted others; and the sighs that Mme. Aubain uttered, as she sat knitting by the window, reached Félicité as she turned her spinning wheel in the kitchen.

They took walks together along the espalier, and talked always about Virginie, wondering whether such and such would have pleased her, or what she would probably have said on this or that occasion.

All her little belongings were in a cupboard in the room

with two beds. Mme. Aubain inspected them as seldom as possible. One summer day she resigned herself to doing so, and moths flew out of the cupboard.

Her dresses were arranged under a shelf on which sat three dolls, some hoops, a doll's house, and the basin that she used daily. They took out her petticoats, stockings, and handkerchiefs and spread them on the two beds, before folding them again. The sun, shining on these pitiful objects, brought out the spots and the creases made by the movements of Virginie's body. Outside the sky was blue, the air was warm, a blackbird warbled. Everything seemed vibrant with a heartfelt sweetness. They found a little hat of deeply piled plush, chestnut-colored; but it was all motheaten. Félicité wanted it for herself. They looked at each other and their eyes filled with tears; at last the mistress opened her arms and the servant threw herself into them. They held each other close, assuaging their grief in a kiss that made them equal.

This was the first time in their lives, for Mme. Aubain was not demonstrative by nature. Félicité was as grateful as if she had been presented with a gift; and from then on she cherished Mme. Aubain with a devotion that was almost animal and with an almost religious veneration.

The kindness of her heart grew.

When she heard in the street the drums of a marching regiment, she stood at the front door with a pitcher of cider and asked the soldiers to drink. She took care of cholera patients. She protected the Poles, and there was even one who wanted to marry her. But they quarreled, for one morning, returning from the Angelus, she found that he had entered her kitchen, prepared a salad, and was nonchalantly eating it.

After the Poles came Papa Colmiche, an old man who was supposed to have been guilty of some atrocities in '93. He lived along the riverbank, in a tumble-down pigsty. The little boys used to spy on him through cracks in the wall and throw stones at him that always landed on the squalid bed where he lay, continually racked by a cough. His hair was long, his eyes inflamed, and on his arm grew a tumor bigger than his head. Félicité supplied him with linen and tried to keep his miserable hut clean. It was her wish to have him installed in the bakehouse without his annoying Madame. When the tumor opened, she dressed it every day. Sometimes she brought him some cake. She used to lay him in the sun on a bed of straw. The poor old fellow, slobbering and shaking, would thank her in his weak voice. He was afraid of losing her, and would stretch out his hand when he saw her going away. He died. She had a mass said for the repose of his soul.

On that day, fortune smiled on her: at the dinner hour, the Negro servant of Mme. de Larsonnière came carrying the parrot in a cage, with perch, chain, and padlock. A note from the baroness informed Mme. Aubain that, because her husband was promoted to a prefecture, they were leaving that evening; and she begged her to accept the bird as a remembrance and a mark of her esteem.

For a long time this bird had occupied Félicité's thoughts, because he came from America and America reminded her of Victor—so much so that she questioned the Negro about that country. Once she had even remarked: "How happy Madame would be to have him!"

The Negro had told this to his mistress, and since she could not take the bird with her, she disposed of him in this fashion.

4

The parrot was called Loulou. His body was green, the tip of his wings pink, his forehead blue, and his throat golden.

But he had the tiresome habit of biting his perch, plucking his feathers, scattering his mess about, and spattering the water of his bath. Mme. Aubain thought the bird was a nuisance and gave him to Félicité to keep.

She set out to train the parrot; soon he could repeat: "Nice boy," "Your servant, sir," "Hello, Mary!" He was placed next to the door, and people were surprised that he would not answer to Jacquot, for weren't all parrots called Jacquot? They likened him to a turkey, to a log of wood; and each time they did so Félicité was hurt to the quick! But Loulou was curiously stubborn! He stopped talking when one looked at him!

Yet he liked company, for on Sunday, while those Rochefeuille ladies, M. de Houppeville, and some new habitués—Onfray the apothecary, M. Varin, and Captain Mathieu—were playing cards, he would beat the window-panes with his wings, and would fling himself about so violently that it was impossible to hear oneself speak.

Bourais' face, undoubtedly, struck him as being very funny. As soon as he spotted Bourais, he would begin to laugh—to laugh with all his might. His noises reverberated through the courtyard, echoes repeated them, the neighbors stood at their windows and laughed too. Therefore, so as not to be seen by the parrot, M. Bourais would slither along the wall, hiding his face under his hat, and, getting down to the river, would enter the house by the garden door. The looks he then shot at the bird were far from tender.

Loulou had been slapped by the butcher boy for taking the liberty of putting his head into the meat basket. Since then, the bird always tried to pinch him through his shirt. Fabu threatened to wring Loulou's neck, although he was not cruel, in spite of his tattooed arms and long sideburns. On the contrary! He was rather fond of the parrot and, in a jovial mood, he even wanted to teach him some curse words. Félicité, alarmed by all these tricks, removed the parrot to the kitchen.

Later, his little chain was removed and he roamed about the house. He would come downstairs by hooking his curved beak on the steps, lifting first his right leg, then his left. Félicité was afraid that all these gymnastics would make the bird dizzy. Sure enough, he did become ill and could neither talk nor eat. There was a thickness under his tongue such as chickens sometimes develop. She cured him by scratching out this thickness with her fingernail.

M. Paul, one day, had the effrontery to blow cigar smoke into the parrot's nostrils. Another time, when Mme. Lormeau was teasing him with the end of her parasol, Loulou snapped at the metal ring. Finally, the bird got lost.

Félicité had put him on the grass to give him some fresh air and had gone away for a minute. When she returned, the parrot was gone! First, she searched in the bushes, then by the riverbank, and on the roofs, paying no attention to her mistress who was screaming, "Be careful! You must be out of your mind!"

Then Félicité looked in all the gardens of Pont l'Évêque, and she stopped everyone passing by—"You haven't seen my parrot, by chance, have you?" To those who did not know the bird, she gave a description. Suddenly, she thought she spotted something green fluttering behind the mill at the bottom of the hill. But when she approached— nothing! A peddler told her he had seen a parrot a little while ago at Saint-Melaine, in Mère Simon's shop. She ran all the way. They didn't know what she was talking about.

Finally, she came home, exhausted, her slippers in shreds, her heart broken by disappointment. As she was sitting on a bench close to Mme. Aubain and was telling her everywhere she had been, a light weight fell on her shoulder. It was Loulou! What the devil had he been doing? Probably taking a stroll in the neighborhood!

Félicité had trouble getting over this—or rather, she never did recover from it.

As a result of a cold, Félicité had an attack of quinsy, and a little later an ear infection. Three years later she was deaf; and she spoke very loud, even in church. Though her sins might have been bruited abroad to all corners of the diocese without shame to her or scandal to anyone, the parish priest thought it best henceforth to hear her confession only in the sacristy.

Imaginary buzzings in the head added to her afflictions. Often her mistress would say to her: "My word, how stupid you are!" She would simply answer, "Yes, Madame," and go look for something to do near her.

The small scope of her ideas became smaller still, and the pealing of the church bells and the lowing of the cattle ceased to exist for her. All living creatures moved about silently as ghosts. The only sound that she could hear now was the voice of the parrot.

As if to distract her, Loulou would mimic the tic-tac of the turnspit, the shrill cry of the the fish vendor, the noise of the carpenter's saw across the road, and when the bell rang, he would imitate Mme. Aubain—"Félicité! The door, the door!"

They had conversations, Loulou incessantly repeating the three short phrases in his repertory, to which Félicité would reply with phrases just as disconnected, but in which there was deep sincerity. Loulou was almost a son and lover to her in her isolated world. He would climb on her fingers, nibble at her lips, and cling to her kerchief; and, when she leaned forward, shaking her head as nurses do, the long wings of her bonnet and those of the bird moved together.

When the clouds were banked on top of one another and

the thunder began to roll, Loulou would utter cries, remembering, perhaps, the downpours in his native forests. Teeming rain made him absolutely mad with joy; he fluttered about wildly, he climbed the ceiling, knocked everything over, and went out through the window to splash in the garden; but he would come back quickly and alight on one of the andirons, and hopping about to dry his feathers, he would show first his tail, then his beak.

One morning in the terrible winter of 1837, when Félicité had put Loulou in front of the fireplace because of the cold, she found him dead, in the center of his cage, his head down, and his claws clutching the wire bars. Undoubtedly, he had died of a congestion. But Félicité thought he had been poisoned with parsley, and despite all lack of evidence, she suspected Fabu.

She wept so bitterly that her mistress said to her: "Well then, have the bird stuffed."

She asked the pharmacist's advice, since he had always been kind to the parrot.

He wrote to LeHavre. A certain man named Fellacher undertook the job. But as parcels sometimes got lost when sent by the stagecoach, she decided to take it herself as far as Honfleur.

Leafless apple trees lined both sides of the road. Ice covered the ditches. Dogs barked on the farms. Félicité, with her hands under her cloak, carrying her basket, and wearing her little black sabots, walked briskly along in the middle of the road.

She went through the forest, passed Haut-Chêne, and reached Saint-Gatien.

Behind her, in a cloud of dust, gathering speed down a steep hill, came a mail coach, with horses at full gallop, like the wind. Seeing this woman who was not paying any attention, the driver stood up, and the postilion shouted, too. All the while the four horses which the driver could not hold back gained speed. The first two horses grazed Félicité. With a pull on the reins, he veered to the side, but, furious, he raised his arm, and in full flight, with his heavy whip he gave her such a lash from her stomach to her neck that she fell on her back.

Her first action, when she regained consciousness, was to open the basket. Fortunately, Loulou was all right. She felt a burning on her right cheek, and when she touched it, her hands were red. The blood was streaming.

She sat down on a pile of stones and dabbed her face with a handkerchief; then she ate a crust of bread which she had put in her basket just in case, and took consolation for her own wound in gazing at the bird.

When she arrived at Ecquemauville, she could see below the lights of Honfleur, which twinkled in the night like a cluster of stars; the sea, beyond, spread out indistinctly. Then weakness forced her to stop; and her wretched childhood, the disillusion of her first love, the departure of her nephew, Virginie's death, all came back to her like the waves of a tide, rising to her throat and choking her.

Later she spoke to the captain of the boat; and without telling him what she was sending, she gave him instructions.

Fellacher kept the parrot a long time. He was always promising it for the following week. At the end of six months he announced it had been dispatched in a box; and then nothing more was heard about it. It seemed that Loulou was never coming back. "They have stolen him from me!" she thought.

Finally he did arrive—and how wonderful he looked, sitting upright on a branch that was screwed to a mahogany base. One foot was held in the air. His head was tilted sidewise, and he was biting on a nut that the taxidermist, carried away by a flair for the grandiose, had painted gold!

Félicité put Loulou in her room.

This place, to which she admitted few, had so many religious objects and so many unusual things that it looked like a chapel and a bazaar combined.

A large wardrobe made it difficult to open the door. Opposite the window overlooking the garden, a small circular window looked down upon the courtyard. On a table near the folding bed stood a water pitcher, two combs, and a bar of blue soap on a chipped plate. On the walls hung rosary beads, medallions, several statues of the Virgin, and a holy water font made of a coconut; on the commode, covered with a cloth like that on altars, stood the box made of shells which Victor had given to her, a watering can, a balloon, some writing books, the geography picture book, and a pair of boots. Fastened by its ribbons to a nail on the mirror hung the small plush hat! Félicité carried this kind of respect to such extremes that she even kept one of Monsieur's frock coats. All the old things Mme. Aubain no longer wanted Félicité took to her room. For this reason there were artificial flowers on the edge of the commode, and a portrait of the Comte d'Artois in the recess of the dormer window.

By means of a small shelf, Loulou was set prominently on the chimney piece that projected into the room. Every morning, when Félicité woke up, she could see him in the dawn's light, and she would recall painlessly and peacefully the old days with their insignificant events down to their last detail.

Communicating with no one, she lived in a kind of sleep-walking trance. The Corpus Christi processions rejuvenated her. She would go to her neighbors begging tapers and mats with which to decorate the altar being erected in the street.

In church she always sat gazing at the stained-glass window that portrayed the Holy Ghost, and noticed there was something of the parrot about it. The resemblance seemed to her more pronounced in a picture that depicted the Baptism of Our Lord. With its purple wings and its emerald body, it was really Loulou's portrait.

She bought this picture and hung it in the place former-ly occupied by the Comte d'Artois—so that, with one glance, she could see them together. They became associ-ated in her mind, the parrot becoming sanctified by this as-sociation with the Holy Ghost, which became more real in her eyes and easier to comprehend. God the Father, to reveal Himself, could not have chosen a dove, since those birds have no voices, but rather one of Loulou's ancestors. And Félicité, although she looked at the picture as she said her prayers, would turn from time to time toward the parrot.

She wanted to join the Ladies of the Blessed Virgin, but Mme. Aubain dissuaded her.

Then a great event occurred: Paul's marriage.

After having been in succession a clerk in a notary's office, in business, in the customs office, in the revenue service, and having even made efforts to get into the bureau of waters and forests—suddenly, at thirty-six, by an inspiration from heaven, he had discovered his career: that of registrar! He showed such aptitude for this kind of work that an inspector had offered him his daughter in marriage, promising to use his influence on Paul's behalf.

Paul, serious-minded now, brought the girl to see his mother.

She sniffed at the ways of Pont-l'Évêque, gave herself the airs of a princess, and hurt Félicité's feelings. Mme. Aubain felt relieved when the visitor left.

The following week news was brought of Bourais' death in an inn in lower Brittany. Rumors of suicide were later confirmed and doubts of his integrity were raised. Mme. Aubain pored over his accounts, and it didn't take her long to discover a long list of his misdeeds: embezzlements, fictitious sales of wood, forged receipts, etc. Besides that, he had an illegitimate child, and "relations with a certain person from Dozulé."

These scandalous acts distressed Madame very much. In March 1853, she was seized with a pain in her chest; her tongue was coated, and leeches did not give her any relief. On the ninth evening she died, having just reached her seventy-second birthday.

Everyone thought she was younger than she really was, because of her brown hair, braids of which framed her pallid, pockmarked face. Few friends regretted her passing, for with her haughty manner she kept people at a distance.

But Félicité mourned her as masters are seldom mourned. That Madame should have died before her disturbed her thoughts, seemed to her contrary to the nature of things, something inadmissible and monstrous.

Ten days later (the time it took to travel from Besançon) the heirs arrived. The daughter-in-law rummaged through drawers, selected certain pieces of furniture, sold the rest. Then they left, and, Paul returned to his registering.

Madame's armchair, her small round table, her foot warmer, the eight chairs were gone! On the walls were yellow squares that marked where pictures used to hang. They had carried off the two beds, with the mattresses, and Virginie's belongings were no longer to be seen in the cupboard! Félicité, numb with sadness, wandered from floor to floor.

Next day there was a notice on the door. The apothecary shouted in her ear that the house was for sale.

She staggered and had to sit down. What distressed her most of all was that she might have to give up her room— so comfortable for poor little Loulou. Gazing at the bird with a look of anguish, she prayed to the Holy Ghost. She had formed the idolatrous habit of saying her prayers on her knees in front of the parrot. Sometimes the sun breaking through the window caught his glass eye, and a long luminous ray would dart from it, throwing Félicité into ecstasy.

She had an income of three hundred and eighty francs a year, willed to her by Mme. Aubain. The garden provided her with vegetables. As for clothes, she had enough to last till the end of her days, and she saved on lighting by going to bed at dusk.

She rarely went out, in order to avoid the secondhand shop where some pieces of the old furniture were displayed for sale. Ever since her shock, she dragged one leg; and as her strength was failing Mère Simon, whose grocery business had fallen into ruin, used to come every morning to chop her wood and pump her water.

Félicité's eyesight became weak.

The shutters of the house would no longer open. Many years passed, but the place was not rented or sold.

For fear of being turned out, Félicité never asked for repairs. The laths of the roof began to rot, so that for a whole year the bolster of her bed was damp. After Easter she began to spit blood.

This time Mère Simon called a doctor. Félicité wanted to know what was the matter with her. But, too deaf to hear, she caught only one word: "Pneumonia." It was familiar enough to her and she answered, softly, "Ah! like Madame," thinking it natural that she should thus follow her mistress.

The time for preparing the altars was nearing. The first of them was always erected at the bottom of the hill, the second in front of the post office, and the third about halfway down the street. There was some difference of opinion concerning this last-mentioned, and the parishioners at last decided to put it in Mme. Aubain's courtyard.

The pain in Félicité's chest and her fever continued to increase. Félicité was annoyed because she could do nothing for the altar. If only she could have at least put something on it. Then she thought of the parrot. But the neighbors objected: it wasn't proper. However, the curé granted permission and this made her so happy that she begged him to accept Loulou, her sole valuable possession, when she died.

From Tuesday to Saturday, the eve of Corpus Christi, she coughed more and more. By the evening, her face was pinched, her lips clung to her gums, and she began to vomit, and next day at early dawn, feeling very weak, she sent for a priest.

Three kindly old women stood around while she received extreme unction. Then she said she wanted to speak to Fabu.

He came in his Sunday clothes, ill at ease in this sad atmosphere.

"Forgive me," she said, with an effort to extend her arm, "I thought it was you who had killed him!"

What did she mean by this nonsense? Suspecting a man like him of being a murderer! He was indignant, and was about to make a scene.

"As you can see, she makes no sense at all."

Every once in a while Félicité would talk to shadows. The three ladies went away and Mère Simon went to breakfast.

A little later Mère Simon took Loulou and, holding him near Félicité, said: "Come, now, say goodbye to him!"

Though he was not a corpse, the worms had begun to devour the dead bird; one of his wings was broken, and the stuffing was coming out of his body. But Félicité, now blind, kissed Loulou's forehead, and pressed him against her cheek. Mère Simon took him away and placed him on the altar.

A scent of summer drifted from the meadow; flies buzzed; the sun made the surface of the river glisten and heated the slate roofs. Mère Simon had come back into the room, and was dozing peacefully.

The tolling of the church bell awakened her; the people were coming from vespers. Félicité's delirium ceased. She thought of the procession, and saw it as if she had been there.

All the children from the schools, the choir singers, together with the firemen, walked along on the pavement, while in the middle of the road marched first the verger armed with his halberd, the beadle carrying his large cross, the schoolmaster watching his small charges, and the sister anxious for her little girls; three of the cutest of these, with curls like angels, were throwing rose petals in the air; the deacon, with his arms outstretched, was leading the music; and two incense bearers bowed at every step in front of the Blessed Sacrament, carried by M. le Curé wearing a beautiful chasuble, beneath a flaming red canopy, held by four churchwardens. Waves of people surged behind, between the white cloths covering the walls of the houses. They arrived at the foot of the hill.

Beads of cold sweat dampened Félicité's temples. Mère Simon sponged them with a piece of cloth, saying to herself that one day she would have to go too.

The murmur of the crowd mounted; for a moment, it was very loud, then it faded.

A fusillade rattled the windowpanes. It was the postilions

saluting the monstrance. Félicité rolled her eyes and said as softly as she could:

"Is he all right?" She was anxiously thinking of her parrot.

Her death agony began. A rattle, more and more violent, shook her sides. Froth appeared at the corners of her mouth and her whole body was trembling.

Soon, above the blaring of the wind instruments, the clear voices of the children and the deep voices of men could be distinguished. At intervals, all was silent, except for the tread of feet shuffling over the strewn flowers, sounding like sheep on the grass.

The priests appeared in the courtyard. Mère Simon climbed on one of the chairs to look through the round window. In this way she could look down upon the altar.

Green wreaths hung from the altar, which was decorated with a flounce of English lace. In the middle there was a small receptacle containing relics; two orange trees stood at the corners, and all along were silver candlesticks and porcelain vases, filled with sunflowers, lilies, peonies, foxgloves, and tufts of hydrangea. This mass of brilliant colors banked from the level of the altar to the rug spread over the pavement. Strange objects caught the eye: a vermilion sugar bowl held a wreath of violets; pendants of Alençon stone glittered on the moss; two Chinese screens depicted landscapes. Loulou, concealed by the roses, showed nothing but his blue forehead, like a piece of lapis lazuli.

The churchwardens, choristers, and children stood in rows on three sides of the courtyard. The priest ascended the steps slowly, and put down his great, shining, golden monstrance on the lacework cloth. All knelt. There was a deep silence; and the censers, swinging to and fro, glided on their little chains.

A blue cloud of smoke rose to Félicité's room. She distended her nostrils, breathing it in with a mystical sensuousness; then she closed her eyes. Her lips were smiling. The beating of her heart became fainter and fainter, softer like an exhausted fountain, like a fading echo; and when she breathed her last breath, she thought she saw in the opening heavens a gigantic parrot, hovering above her head.

The Legend of St. Julian
the Hospitaler

1

Julian's father and mother lived in a castle, surrounded by a forest, on the slope of a hill.

The towers at each of the four corners had pointed roofs covered with scales of lead, and the walls rested on huge slabs of rock, which dropped abruptly to the bottom of the moat.

The pavement of the courtyard was as clean as the flagstones of a church. Long rainspouts, shaped like dragons with their heads down, spat rainwater into the cistern; and on the window ledges of every story, in painted earthenware pots, bloomed either basil or heliotrope.

A second enclosure, fenced with stakes, contained first an orchard of fruit trees, then a garden in symmetrical patterns, next trellis-covered arbors where one could sit to enjoy the fresh air, and, last, a mall where the pages played their games. On the other side were the barns, the kennels, the stables, the bakery, and the wine presses. A pasture of green grass, spread all around these, was itself enclosed by a thick, thorny hedge.

They had lived in peace for so long that the portcullis was never lowered; the moats were full of water; swallows made their nests in the cracks of the battlements; and the guard, a bowman who customarily paced back and forth all day long, entered his watchtower, when the sun blazed too hot, and slept like a monk.

Inside the castle, ironwork gleamed everywhere; tapestries hung in the rooms for protection against the cold; cupboards overflowed with linen; wine casks were piled in the cellars, where oaken chests were splitting under the weight of moneybags.

In the armory, between standards and mounted heads of wild beasts, could be seen weapons of all ages and of all nations, from the slings of the Amalekites and the javelins of the Garamantes, to the scimitars of the Saracens and the coats of mail of the Normans.

The chief spit in the kitchen was strong enough to turn an ox. The chapel was as sumptuous as a king's oratory. There was even, in a place apart, a Roman vapor bath, but the good seigneur abstained from using it, considering that this was a heathen practice.

Wrapped always in his foxskin robes, he walked about his castle, administering justice among his vassals, even settling the quarrels of his neighbors. During the winter, he would watch the snowflakes falling or would have stories read to him. With the first fine days of spring, he rode his mule along the byways, beside his greening cornfields, and chatted with the peasants, giving them counsel.

After many youthful adventures, he took for a wife a damsel of high lineage. Very fair she was, a little proud and serious. The points of her coif brushed the lintels of the doors, the train of her dress flowed three paces behind her. Her household was ordered like the inside of a monastery; each morning she would assign work to the servants and inspect the making of preserves or unguents. She herself worked at her spinning wheel or embroidered altar linens. By dint of her prayers to God, a son was born to her.

Then there was great rejoicing and feasting, which lasted for three days and four nights—nights made bright by torches, whose flames glistened on leaves and flowers, while harps made music. They ate the rarest spices on fowl as large as sheep; for amusement, a dwarf came out of a pie; and, as there were not enough bowls to go around—for the crowd grew greater and greater—they were obliged to drink from horns and helmets.

The new mother was not present at these festivities. She stayed quietly in her bed. One evening, she awoke and saw under a moonbeam that came through the window what she thought was a moving shadow. It was an old man in sackcloth, with a chaplet at his side, a beggar's bag hung over his shoulder. He had every appearance of being a hermit. He approached her pillow and said to her, without opening his lips, "Rejoice, O mother! Thy son shall be a saint."

She was about to cry out, but, as if gliding on the moonbeam, he rose gently into the air and vanished. The singing at the banquet rang out more loudly. She heard angels' voices; and her head fell back on the pillow, over which, in a frame of garnets, hung a martyr's bone.

The next morning all the servants were questioned and each declared that he had not seen the hermit. Dream or reality, it must have been a message from heaven; but she was careful to say nothing more about it, fearing she might be accused of pride.

The guests left at dawn, and while Julian's father was outside the postern gate, through which he had just escorted the last guest, suddenly a beggar stood before him, in the mist. It was a fiery-eyed gypsy, with plaited beard, and he wore silver rings on both arms. As if inspired, he stammered these disconnected words: "Ah! Ah! Your son! . . . Much blood! . . . Much glory! . . . Always Happy! An emperor's family."

And bending over to pick up his alms, he disappeared and was lost in the grass.

The good lord of the manor looked right and left, and called as loudly as he could. No one! The wind blew, the morning mist lifted.

He attributed this vision to a head weary from too little sleep. "If I speak of this, they will laugh at me," he said to himself. Yet the glory destined for his son dazzled him, although the promise was not clear, and he even doubted if he had heard it.

Husband and wife kept their secrets from each other. But both cherished their son with an equal love; and, revering him as one chosen by God, they were infinitely concerned for his person. His bed was stuffed with the softest down; a lamp in the form of a dove burned above it continually; three nurses rocked him to sleep; and, carefully wrapped in his swaddling clothes, inside his brocaded cloak, with his rosy complexion and blue eyes, looking out beneath a bonnet laden with pearls, he resembled a little Jesus. He teethed without once crying.

When he was seven, his mother taught him to sing. To make him brave his father hoisted him on the back of a huge horse. The child smiled gleefully, and soon knew everything about chargers.

A wise old monk taught him the Holy Scriptures, Arabic numbers, Latin, and how to paint delicately on vellum. They worked together, high up in a tower, away from the noises of the castle.

Lessons over, they went down to the garden, where, walking along slowly, they studied the flowers.

Sometimes they saw, wending through the valley below, a file of beasts of burden, led by an unmounted man in Oriental garb. The lord, recognizing him to be a merchant, sent a servant to him, and the stranger, heartened, turned off his road. And, being shown into the parlor, he took from his chests pieces of silk and velvet, jewels, perfumes, and curios whose uses were unknown. Finally the tradesman left with a goodly profit, having suffered no violence. At other times, a band of pilgrims knocked at the gate. Their wet garments steamed before the fire; and, when they had been well fed, they told of their travels: of sailing over foamy seas, of journeys on foot over burning desert sands, of the cruelty of the pagans, of the caves of Syria, and of the Manger and the Sepulcher. Then they gave to the young seigneur shells from the pockets of their cloaks.

Often the lord of the manor regaled his old companions-at-arms. As they drank, they would recall the wars, the storming of fortresses with jarring machines, and the gaping wounds. Julian, who was listening to them, would shout out; and then his father did not doubt that someday Julian would be a conqueror. Yet, at evening time, at the end of the Angelus, as he passed among the kneeling poor, he would dip into his purse so modestly, and yet so nobly, that his mother thought surely to see Julian someday an archbishop.

His place in chapel was beside his parents; and, however long the services, he remained kneeling on his *prie-dieu,* his hands reverently joined, and his cap on the floor.

One day, during mass, he saw, as he raised his head, a little white mouse scurrying from a hole in the wall. It scampered along the first step of the altar, and, after two or three turns to the right and left, fled whence it came. The following Sunday, the thought that he might see it again troubled him. It did come again; and every Sunday he waited for it, was annoyed by it, was seized with hatred for it, and determined to rid himself of it.

So, having closed the door and having sprinkled some cake crumbs on the altar steps, he posted himself in front of the hole, with a stick in his hand.

After a very long time a small pink nose appeared, then the whole mouse. He struck a slight blow, and stood aghast over this tiny body which no longer moved. A drop of blood stained the flagstone. He wiped it away quickly with his sleeve, threw the mouse outside, and said nothing to anyone.

All kinds of little birds picked up seeds in the garden. Julian thought of putting dry peas into a hollow reed. When he heard warbling in a tree, he stealthily approached, lifted his pipe, and puffed out his cheeks. So many little dead creatures rained down on his shoulders that he laughed, delighted with his malice.

One morning, as Julian was returning along the castle wall, he spied on the top of the rampart a fat pigeon, preening itself in the sun. He stopped to look at it, and, as there was a breach in the wall at that place, a stone chip lay ready to his hand. He swung his arm, and the stone struck the bird, which fell headlong into the moat.

He hurried to the bottom of the ditch, tearing himself among the briars and searching everywhere, friskier than a puppy. The pigeon, its wings broken, quivered on a branch of privet.

Its persistent will to live irritated the child. He began to strangle it; the bird's writhings made his heart thump, filling him with a savage, tumultuous delight. When at last it stiffened, he felt faint.

That night, during supper, his father declared that it was time for him to learn the art of venery; so he went to look for an old manuscript, containing, in question-and-answer form, lessons on all the phases of hunting. A master therein explained to his pupil the art of training dogs, of taming falcons, and of setting traps; how to recognize the spoors—of the stag by its droppings, of the fox by its footprints, of the wolf by its scratches on the ground; how properly to spot their trails, and where their lairs are usually found, how to rouse them; to know what winds are the most favorable; and to memorize a list of game calls and rules of disposing of the quarry.

When Julian could recite all this by heart, his father assembled a pack of dogs for him.

First of all, there were twenty-four Barbary greyhounds, speedier than gazelles, but apt to get out of hand; then seventeen pairs of Breton dogs, red with white spots, heavy-chested, loud of voice, and superb in obedience. For attacking the wild boar, after following it in its dangerous doublings, there were forty boarhounds, shaggy as bears. Mastiffs from Tartary, almost as tall as donkeys, flame-colored, with broad backs and straight legs, were chosen to chase aurochs. The black coats of the spaniels had the sheen of satin, and the yelping of the talbots was equal to the singing of the beagles. In a yard by themselves, straining at their chains and rolling their eyes, growled eight alan dogs, formidable beasts that jump at the bellies of horsemen, and have no fear of lions.

All ate wheat bread, drank from stone troughs, and bore sonorous names.

The falcons, perhaps, were even more fiery than the dogs. The good seigneur, by dint of his wealth, had procured tercelets from the Caucasus, sakers from Babylon, gyrfalcons from Germany, and peregrines captured on the cliffs, at the edge of cold seas, in faraway lands. They were quartered in a thatch-roofed shed, and, fastened to a perch in the order of their height, they had before them a heap of turf on which they were placed from time to time to exercise.

Purse-nets, hooks, wolf-traps, and all kinds of snares were made.

Often they took into the country bird dogs, which quickly came to point. Then the hunters, advancing step by step, cautiously stretched over their motionless bodies a large net. At a command, the dogs barked; the quail flew up; and the ladies of the neighborhood, invited to the hunt with their husbands, their children, and servants— everyone dashed for the net and easily caught the birds.

At other times, to start up the hares, they would beat drums; foxes were lured into pits, or a trap would spring and catch a wolf by the paw.

But Julian disdained these convenient artifices; he preferred to hunt, with his horse and falcon, far from the crowd. His favorite was almost always a large Scythian tartaret, white as snow. His leather hood was topped with a plume, gold bells jangled on his blue feet, and he held firmly to his master's arm while the horse galloped and the plains rolled away beneath them. Julian, unhooding him and untying his jesses, suddenly let him go; the daring bird rose straight into the air like an arrow. Then Julian saw two specks of unequal size wheel in flight, come together, and then disappear into the high blue reaches. The falcon soon came down, tearing some bird, and, his wings fluttering, perched again on Julian's gantlet.

Julian hunted the heron, the kite, the crow, and the vulture in this way.

He loved to sound his hunting horn and to follow his dogs as they leaped over the hillsides, jumped the streams, and bounded toward the woods.

When a stag began to pant under their savage attacks, Julian would adroitly knock him down, and then take delight in the fury with which the mastiffs devoured him, tearing to pieces his bleeding skin.

When days were misty, he hid himself in the marshes to wait for geese, wild duck, or otters.

At dawn, three equerries waited for him at the foot of the steps, and though the old monk, leaning from his window, entreated him to come back, Julian would not. He went out in the heat of the sun, in the rain, in stormy weather; he drank spring water from his hand, ate wild apples as he jogged along, rested under an oak if he was fatigued. He returned to the château very late at night, with thorns in his hair, covered with blood and mud, and reeking with the odor of wild beasts. He became like them. When his mother kissed him, he received her embrace coldly, but his thoughts seemed to be far away.

He slew bears with a stroke of the knife, bulls with the ax, and wild boars with the spear; and once, armed with nothing but a stick, even defended himself against wolves that were gnawing corpses at the foot of a gibbet.

One winter morning, Julian started out before daybreak, all equipped, with a crossbow over his shoulder and a quiver of arrows at his saddlebow.

His Danish jennet, followed by two bassets, galloping along at an even pace, made the ground resound. Flakes of frost clung to his cloak; a biting wind howled. On one side, the horizon was brightening; and in the pale light of dawn, he saw rabbits hopping near their warrens. Instantly the two bassets were after them, and here and there quickly broke their backs.

Soon he entered a wood. On a branch of a fallen tree, a grouse, stiff with cold, slept with its head under its wing. With a backward blow of his sword, Julian cut off its two feet, and without stopping to pick it up, continued on his way.

Three hours later, he was on the ridge of a mountain so high that the sky seemed almost black. Below him, on the edge of a high precipice above a ravine, stood two wild goats, looking down into the chasm. As he did not then have his arrows, having left his horse behind, he thought he would go down to them; so, barefoot, and bending over, he managed to stalk the first of them, and plunged a dagger into its side. The second, frightened, leaped into the chasm. Julian slid after it, intending to strike it; but, slipping on his right foot, he fell across the body of the first goat, with his head facing over the precipice and his arms spread apart.

He came down again into the plain and followed the willows that bordered the river. Cranes, flying very low, passed overhead from time to time. Julian killed them with his whip, not missing a single one.

Meanwhile the warmer air had melted the frost; drifts of fog floated around him, until the sun appeared. Then, in the distance, he could see a silvery, still lake gleaming. In the middle of it, there was an animal Julian did not then recognize—a black-nosed beaver. Despite the distance, he felled it with an arrow; and was disappointed because he could not carry off the skin.

Then he wended his way down an avenue of tall trees whose tops formed a sort of triumphal arch to the entrance of a forest. A roebuck bounded from a thicket, a fallow deer appeared at a crossing, a badger came out of a hole, a peacock, in a green clearing, spread its tail; and when he had killed them all, more roebuck, deer, badgers, peacocks, blackbirds, jays, polecats, foxes, hedgehogs, lynxes, an infinite variety of birds and beasts appeared. Trembling, they moved about him, with glances full of gentleness and supplication. But Julian never tired of killing—by turns bending his crossbow, thrusting with his sword, striking with his cutlass—he gave no thought to anything; he had no memory of anything whatsoever. He only knew that he was hunting in some region or other, for an indefinite time, where everything was done with the ease one experiences in dreams. An unusual sight arrested him. Stags filled a valley shaped like an amphitheater; they were packed close against each other, warming one another with their body heat. Their breath could be seen steaming in the mist.

For several minutes, the certainty of a great slaughter, suffocated him with joy. Then he dismounted, rolled back his sleeves, and began to shoot.

At the zing of the first arrow, all the stags turned their heads at once; soon there were gaps in their mass; plaintive cries arose, and undirected movement stirred the herd.

The rim of the valley was too steep to climb. They leaped about in this enclosure looking for the way to escape. Julian aimed and shot, the arrows falling like the shafts of a torrential rain. The maddened stags fought, reared, climbed on each other's backs; the bodies and entangled antlers made a huge heap that crumbled as they changed position.

At last they lay dead on the sand, frothing at their nostrils, entrails protruding, but the heaving of their bodies subsided by degrees. Then all was quiet.

Night was falling, and behind the woods one saw, between the boughs, the sky red as a sheet of blood.

Julian leaned with his back against a tree. He gazed with staring eyes at the enormity of the massacre, unable to comprehend what he had wrought.

Then on the other side of the valley, on the edge of the forest, he saw a stag, with its hind and fawn.

The stag, black and monstrously tall, had sixteen points and a white beard. The hind, blond as dead leaves, was grazing, and, without interfering with her movements, suckled her spotted fawn.

Once more the crossbow twanged. The fawn fell instantly. Thereupon its mother, with her head lifted skyward, bleated with a deep, heartbreaking human voice. In exasperation Julian laid her on the ground with an arrow straight to her heart.

The huge stag saw the hunter and jumped. Julian shot his last arrow. It caught him in the forehead and stayed fixed there.

The great stag seemed not to feel it; but, leaping over the dead bodies, he moved steadily forward. He was about to charge Julian and rip him open; but Julian retreated in indescribable terror. The monstrous beast stopped, eyes flaming, and, as solemn as a patriarch or judge, repeated three times, while a bell tolled in the distance: "Accursed!

Accursed! Accursed! One day, O vicious heart, thou shalt murder thy father and mother!"

The stag's knees bent, his eyes closed gently, and he died.

Julian was dazed, then suddenly overwhelmed with fatigue; disgust and melancholy filled his heart. With his head buried in his hands, he wept for a long time.

His horse was lost; his dogs had left him; the loneliness that enshrouded him seemed to threaten with vague perils. Driven by terror, he fled across the countryside, chose a path at random, and found himself almost immediately at the castle gate.

He did not sleep at night. Beneath the flickering of the hanging lamps, he always saw the great black stag. Its prophecy obsessed him; he struggled against it. "No! No! I could not kill them!" Then he thought, "But suppose I wanted to? . . ." And he feared that the devil might instill in him the desire.

For three months his mother prayed by his bedside in anguish, and his father, moaning, paced the corridor day and night. He sent for the most famous master physicians, who prescribed quantities of drugs. Julian's illness, they said, was caused by an ill wind, or a desire for love. But the young man, to all their questions, shook his head.

His strength, at length reviving, the old monk and the good seigneur, each supporting him with an arm, took him walking in the courtyard.

When he had fully recovered, he persistently refused to hunt.

His father, wishing to please him, made him a present of a long Saracen sword. This was placed on the top of a pillar, in a stand of arms. A ladder was needed to reach it. Julian climbed the ladder. The sword was so heavy that it slipped from his fingers, and, in falling, brushed the good seigneur so closely that his coat was torn. Julian, thinking he had killed his father, fainted.

For a long time thereafter he dreaded arms. He paled at the sight of an unsheathed sword. This weakness distressed his family.

At last the old monk, in the name of God, his honor, and his ancestors, bade him take up the exercises of a gentleman.

The equerries amused themselves daily practicing with the javelin. Julian was quick to excel in this sport: he could hurl his javelin into the neck of a bottle, break the teeth of a weather vane, and hit the nails of the gate at a hundred paces.

One summer evening, at the hour when mist makes things indistinct, he was under the trellis in the garden and saw at the far end two white wings fluttering about at the top of the espalier. He did not doubt but that it was a stork, and he threw his javelin.

A piercing cry rang out.

It was his mother, whose bonnet with its long flaps had been nailed to the wall.

Julian fled from the château, and never returned.

2

He joined a passing company of adventurers.

He came to know hunger and thirst, fevers and vermin. He grew accustomed to the noise of battles, and to the sight of dying men. Sun and wind tanned his skin. Armor hardened his limbs; and, as he was very strong, brave, temperate, and clever, he easily obtained command of a company.

When the battle began, he would lead his soldiers forward with a mighty gesture of his sword. With a knotted rope, swinging in the wind, he scaled the walls of fortresses at night, while sparks of Greek fire struck to his cuirass and boiling resin and molten lead streamed from the battlements. Often a hurled stone dented his buckler. Bridges under the weight of too many men gave way beneath him. With a swing of his mace, he could get rid of fourteen horsemen. In the lists he defied all challengers. More than twenty times everyone thought him dead.

Thanks to Divine favor, he always escaped, for he protected churchmen, orphans, widows, and especially the old. When he saw an aged man walking in front of him, Julian would challenge him to show his face, as if he were afraid of killing him by mistake.

Runaway slaves, rebellious peasants, fortuneless bastards, and all kinds of dauntless men rallied under his banner; thus he formed an army.

It grew and Julian became famous. He was sought after.

One after another he succored the Dauphin of France and the King of England, the Templars of Jerusalem, the

Surena of the Parthians, the Negus of Abyssinia, and the
Emperor of Calicut. He fought the Scandinavians covered
with their fish scales; Negroes, armed with round bucklers
of hippopotamus hide; and gold-colored Indians, mounted
on red asses, who brandished above their diadems broad
sabers, brighter than mirrors. He vanquished the Troglo-
dytes and the Anthropophagi. He traveled regions so hot
that, beneath the scorching sun, hair blazed like torches;
and other regions so cold that the arms snapped from the
body and fell to the ground; and countries where there was
so much fog that people walked surrounded by phantoms.

Republics in political difficulties consulted him. When
negotiating with ambassadors, he obtained unhoped-for
terms. If a monarch behaved too badly, Julian would suddenly arrive and remonstrate. He set nations free and
delivered queens imprisoned in towers. It was he, and no
other, who slew the serpent of Milan and the dragon of
Oberbirbach.

Now the Emperor of Occitania, having triumphed over
the Spanish Moslems, had taken as his concubine the sister
of the Caliph of Cordova; he had a daughter by her, whom
he had raised as a Christian. But the Caliph, pretending
to desire to be converted, came to pay him a visit, attended
by a numerous escort. He massacred the entire garrison,
and threw the Emperor into an underground dungeon,
where he was treated harshly so that the Caliph might
extort his treasures.

Julian hastened to the Emperor's aid, destroyed the
army of the infidels, besieged the city, killed the Caliph,
cut off his head, and hurled it like a ball over the ramparts.
Then he rescued the Emperor from his prison and restored
him to his throne in the presence of the whole court.

The Emperor, as a reward for his service, set before
him baskets full of money; Julian wanted none of it. Thinking that he wanted more, the Emperor offered him three-
quarters of his wealth; again a refusal; then, a share of his
kingdom; Julian thanked him; and the Emperor shed tears
of distress, not knowing how to show his gratitude, when
suddenly he struck his forehead and whispered something

to a page; the tapestry curtains were drawn, and a maiden appeared.

Her large black eyes shone like two soft lamps. A charming smile parted her lips. The ringlets of her hair were caught in the jewels of her partly opened bodice; and, beneath her transparent tunic, one could easily surmise the youthful beauty of her body. She was very dainty and soft, and slender at the waist.

Julian was bedazzled with love, especially since he had lived hitherto a very chaste life.

So he took in marriage the Emperor's daughter; as dowry there was a castle she held from her mother; and, when the wedding and a profusion of courtesies were exchanged, they departed.

The bride's palace was of white marble, constructed in the Moorish style, on a promontory, in a grove of orange trees. Flowered terraces sloped to the beach of a bay, where pink shells cracked under foot. Behind the castle stretched a forest shaped like a fan. The sky was always blue, and the trees swayed either from the sea breeze or the wind from the mountains, which reached to the distant horizon.

The rooms, full of twilight, were lighted by torches partly concealed by the incrustations on the walls. High columns, slender as reeds, supported the vaulted cupolas, decorated in relief by figures imitating the stalactites in caverns.

In the larger rooms, there were water fountains, festooned partitions, a thousand refinements of architecture, and everywhere such sweet silence that one could hear the rustling of a scarf or the echo of a sigh when one entered the courtyard paved with mosaics.

Julian no longer made war. He rested, surrounded by peaceful people; and every day, a crowd passed before him, making obeisance and kissing his hands in the Eastern fashion.

In purple robes, he would remain leaning in the embrasure of a window, recalling his hunts of former days. He would have liked to chase over the desert after gazelles and ostriches, or to hide among the bamboo plants waiting for leopards, or to travel through forests filled with rhinoceroses, or to climb to the almost inaccessible mountain-tops to take better aim at eagles, or to fight the white bears on the ice floes of some far northern sea.

Sometimes, in dreams, he saw himself like our father Adam in Paradise, among all the beasts; by stretching his arm, he made them to die, or else they paraded before him, two by two, in order of size, from the elephants and the lions to the ermines and the ducks, as on the day when they entered Noah's Ark. From the shadow of a cave, he hurled javelins at them that never missed; other animals appeared; there was no end to them; and then he woke, his eyes rolling wildly.

Princes who were his friends invited him to hunt. Always he refused, thinking that, by this penance, he would avert his evil fate; for it seemed to him that the fate of his parents depended somehow on his slaughtering or not slaughtering animals. But he suffered from not seeing them, and his other longing—to hunt—became unbearable.

His wife, to amuse him, sent for jugglers and dancers.

She rode with him in an open litter through the country; at other times, lying in a boat, they would watch the fish darting about in water clear as the sky. Often she would pelt his face with flowers; or, sitting at his feet, she would strum songs on a three-stringed mandolin; then, placing her clasped hands on his shoulder, she would say timidly, "What is the matter, my dear lord?"

He would not answer, but would burst into sobs. One day, he did confess to her his horrible fear.

She fought it, arguing very convincingly: his father and mother, most probably, were dead; if ever he should see them again, by chance, for whatever reason, would he commit this abomination? Therefore, his fears were groundless, and he should hunt again.

Julian smiled as he listened to her, but could not decide to satisfy his desire.

One evening in the month of August, when they were in their room, she had just retired to bed and Julian was praying on his knees. Suddenly, he heard the yelping of a fox, then light footsteps under his window; and he saw in the shadows what seemed like shapes of animals. The temptation was too strong. He took down his quiver.

His wife seemed surprised.

"I go to obey you," he said, "At sunrise, I shall return."

However, she feared some terrible adventure.

He comforted her, then left, surprised by the inconsistency of her moods.

Soon afterward, a page came to announce two strangers, who, in the absence of the lord of the manor, requested to see her ladyship.

Soon there entered the room an old man and an old woman, stooped and dusty, clad in coarse garments, each leaning on a staff.

They took courage and said they came to bring Julian news about his parents.

She leaned forward on her bed to listen.

But, having consulted each other with a glance, they asked her if he still loved them, if he ever spoke of them.

"Oh yes! Yes!" she replied.

Then they cried, "Well, we are they." And they sat down, very weary, overcome with fatigue.

But nothing was there to assure the young wife that her husband was their son.

They gave proof by describing certain marks he had on his skin.

She sprang out of bed, called her page, and a repast was served to them.

Although they were very hungry, they could scarcely eat, and she observed furtively the trembling of their bony hands as they grasped their goblets.

A thousand questions about Julian were posed. She answered every one, but was careful not to say anything about the terrible prophecy that concerned them.

When Julian did not return, they had left their château, and wandered for many years, following vague clues, without losing hope. So much money was spent on toll bridges and inns, on the dues of princes and the demands of thieves, that their purse was empty, and now they were reduced to begging. But what did it matter, as they would soon embrace their son? They extolled his good fortune in having so sweet a wife, and did not tire of gazing at her and kissing her.

The luxury of the apartment surprised them greatly, and the old man, having scrutinized the walls, asked why the coat of arms of Occitania's Emperor hung there.

"He is my father!" she replied.

Thereupon he started, remembering the gypsy's prophecy, while the old woman thought of the hermit's words. Doubtless this present glory of her son was only the dawn of eternal splendor. Both sat, completely entranced, beneath the light from the candelabra on the table.

They must have been very handsome in their youth. The mother still had all her hair; its fine locks drifted like snow about her face; and the father, with his tall figure and his long beard, resembled a statue in a church.

Julian's wife urged them not to wait for him. She gave them her own bed, then closed the casement window. They fell asleep. It was almost daybreak, and outside the window, little birds were beginning to sing.

Julian had crossed the park and was walking spiritedly through the forest, enjoying the softness of the grass and the fragrance in the air.

Shadows of the trees crept across the moss. Sometimes, moonlight made white patches in the clearing, and he hesitated to go forward, thinking he saw a pool of water; or, sometimes the still surface of a pond would blend with the color of the grass. Everywhere there was deep silence; and he saw none of the beasts that, a few minutes before, were wandering around his castle.

The woods grew more dense, the darkness deeper. Puffs of warm wind, full of enervating odors, caressed his cheeks. He sank his feet in heaps of dead leaves, and leaned against an oak to catch his breath.

Suddenly, from behind him, a black mass sprang; it was a wild boar. Julian had no time to seize his bow, and he grieved over that as if at a calamity.

Then, when he had left the woods, he spied a wolf slinking along a hedge.

Julian shot an arrow at him. The wolf stopped, turned to look at him, and went on. The animal trotted on but, keeping always the same distance, stopped from time to time; but as soon as Julian would aim, he would take flight again.

Walking on, Julian crossed a wide plain, then ridges of sand hills, and found himself at last upon a plateau that overlooked a vast stretch of country. Flat stones were scattered about among ruined crypts. He stumbled over dead men's bones; here and there, worm-eaten crosses leaned sadly askew. But vague shapes moved about in the shadows of the tombs; and hyenas rose out of them, terrified and panting. They moved toward him, their claws clattering on the flagstones; they sniffed at him and, yawning, showed their gums. He unsheathed his sword. They ran off in all directions at once and disappeared with their rapid, limping gallop, beyond a cloud of dust in the distance.

An hour later, in a ravine, he met a savage bull, with horns lowered and hoofs pawing the sand. Julian speared him under the dewlap. His lance broke as if the animal were made of bronze; he closed his eyes, waiting for death. When he opened them, the bull had disappeared.

Then his heart sank for shame. A superior power was destroying his strength; and he turned back into the forest to return home.

Creeping vines tangled around his feet, and he was cutting them with his saber when a marten suddenly slipped between his legs; a panther bounded over his shoulder, and a snake coiled around an ash tree. From its branches a monstrous jackdaw looked down at Julian, and here and there, between the branches, there appeared a galaxy of great sparks, as if the firmament had rained on the forest all its stars. They were the eyes of animals: wildcats, squirrels, owls, parrots, and monkeys.

Julian shot arrows at them; the feathered shafts rested on the leaves like white butterflies. He threw stones at them; they fell without touching anything. He cursed himself, wanted to fight, shouted imprecations; he choked with rage.

Then all the animals that he had hunted reappeared and formed a tight circle around him. Some sat on their haunches, others stood erect. Julian, in their midst, was frozen with terror, incapable of the slightest movement. With a supreme effort of will, he took a step; those perched in the trees fluttered their wings; those on the ground stretched their limbs; and all escorted him.

The hyenas walked in front, the wolf and the wild boar behind. The bull on his right kept swaying his head, and on the left the serpent glided through the grass, while the panther, arching her back, advanced with long, velvety strides. Julian walked as slowly as he could to avoid irritating them. He saw porcupines, foxes, vipers, jackals, and bears emerge from the dense thickets.

When Julian began to run, they ran. The serpent hissed, the stinking beasts foamed. The wild boar's tusks nudged his heels, the wolf's hairy nose sniffed his palms. The monkeys, grimacing, pinched him; the marten rolled at his feet. A bear, with a backward blow of his paw, knocked his hat off; and the panther, disdainfully, dropped at his feet the arrow she had been carrying in her mouth.

All their movements seemed ironical. As they watched him furtively, they seemed to be planning vengeance; while he, deafened by the buzzing of insects, beaten by the wings of birds, and suffocated by the breath of animals, walked with eyes closed and with arms outstretched, like a blind man, without strength enough to cry, "Mercy!"

The crow of a cock rang through the air. Others answered: it was morning, and Julian recognized above the orange trees the roof of his palace.

Then, at the edge of a field, he saw, three paces from him, red partridges fluttering in the stubble. He unfastened his cloak and threw it over them like a net. When he uncovered them, he found but one, and that had been dead a long while and was decayed.

This mockery infuriated him more than all the others.

His thirst for slaughter took possession of him again, and, for want of beasts, he longed to slaughter men.

He climbed the three terraces and burst open the door with his fist. But at the foot of the staircase, the memory of his dear wife calmed his troubled spirit. No doubt she was sleeping, and he would surprise her.

Removing his sandals, he turned the knob softly and entered their bedroom.

The leaded window dimmed the pale light of the dawn. Julian stumbled over clothing on the floor; a little farther on, he bumped against the credence table still laden with dishes. "Doubtless, she has eaten," he said to himself; and he made his way toward the bed, which was lost in the darkness at the end of the room. When he was beside it, in order to kiss his wife, he leaned over the pillow on which lay two heads side by side. Then he felt the touch of a beard against his mouth.

He drew back, thinking he had gone mad, but approached the bed again. As he felt about, his fingers touched long hair. To convince himself that he was wrong, he slowly passed his hand again over the pillow. This time it was indeed a beard! A man! A man in bed with his wife!

With an uncontrollable burst of fury, he leaped upon them, striking with his dagger; he stamped and fumed like a beast gone mad. Then he stopped. The bodies, pierced to the heart, had not even moved. He listened attentively to the two almost uniform death rattles; and as they grew weaker, another, in the far distance, followed them. Indistinct at first, this plaintive, long-drawn voice came nearer, swelled, rang cruelly, and Julian, terrified, recognized the braying of the great black stag.

And as he turned around, he thought he saw framed in the doorway the ghost of his wife, with a light in her hand.

The commotion had awakened her. With one sweeping glance, she understood it all, and fled in horror, dropping her torch.

He picked it up.

His father and mother lay before him, stretched on their backs, each with a wound in the breast; and their faces, majestic in their gentleness, seemed to be guarding an eternal secret. Splashes and pools of blood were on their white skin, on the bed linen, on the floor, even on an ivory Christ hanging in the recess. The scarlet reflection from the stained-glass window, at that moment struck by the sun, intensified these red spots and scattered others throughout the room. Julian walked toward the two bodies, muttering to himself and trying to believe that this was not possible, that he was mistaken, that one sometimes finds inexplicable resemblances. Finally, he bent over to look at the old man more closely, and he saw between the half-closed eyelids a staring eye that burned him like fire. Then he went to the other side of the bed, occupied by the other body, whose white hair concealed a part of the face. Julian slipped his fingers under the hair, raised the head, and gazed at it, holding it at the end of his outstretched arm, while with the other hand he raised the torch to throw more light on it. Drops of blood soaked the mattress and fell one by one to the floor.

At the end of the day, he appeared before his wife; and, in a voice not his own, he bade her, first of all, not to answer him, not to come near him, not even to look at him, and to follow, under pain of damnation, all his orders, which would be irrevocable.

The obsequies were to be carried out according to written instructions he had left on a *prie-dieu* in the chamber of the dead. He abandoned to her the palace, his vassals, and all his possessions, not even keeping for himself the clothes that covered his body, nor his sandals, which she would find at the top of the stairs.

She had obeyed God's Will by making his crime possible, and she must pray for his soul, since henceforward he would cease to exist.

The dead were buried with pomp in a chapel of a monastery three days' journey from the castle. A monk with his cowl lowered followed the procession, at a distance far from all the rest, and no one dared speak to him.

He remained during the mass lying prostrate in the middle doorway, his arms outstretched in the form of a cross, and his forehead in the dust.

After the burial, he was seen taking a road that led to the mountains. He turned around several times to look, and finally disappeared.

3

Julian went abroad, begging his way.

He held out his hand to riders on highways, and bent his knee when he approached harvesters, or stood motionless before the gates of courtyards, his face so sad that no one ever refused him alms.

When, in a spirit of humility, he told his story, all fled from him, making the sign of the cross. When he reentered a village, as soon as he was recognized, the people closed their doors, shouted abuses at him, and hurled stones. The most charitable among them placed a bowl on the window sill, then closed the shutters in order not to see him.

As he was rejected everywhere, he avoided the company of men and lived on roots, plants, wild fruits; also on shellfish, which he gathered along the beaches.

Sometimes, at the bend of a hill road, he saw before his eyes a jumble of crowded roofs, towers, some stone spires, bridges, dark streets crisscrossing, from which rose to his ears a ceaseless humming.

The need to mingle with the life of others impelled him to go down into the town. But the bestial expression on the people's faces, their noisy occupations and trivial conversations left his heart cold. At dawn on feast days, when the cathedral bells lifted the spirits of the whole people, he watched them come from their houses. He saw dancing in the public squares, beer fountains at the street corners, damask hung before the lodging of princes, and, at eventide, through the windows on the ground floor, he saw long family tables where loving grandparents held their grandchildren on their knees. Then sobs choked him, and he turned away and went back to the country.

With transports of love he gazed at young colts frisking in the grass, at birds in their nests, at insects on the flowers; but, at his approach, they all fled, hid in terror, or flew swiftly away.

He sought solitude. But the wind carried to his ears sounds like a death rattle; the tears of dew glistening on plants recalled to his mind heavier drops. Every evening, the sun tinted the clouds with blood, and every night, in his dreams, he reenacted the murder of his parents.

He made himself a hair shirt with iron points. He climbed on his knees to the top of every hill where there was a chapel. But his bitter thoughts darkened the splendor of cathedrals and tortured him despite his penitential mortifications.

He did not rebel against God for having assigned that deed to him, but he despaired because he had been capable of committing it.

His own person filled him with such horror that, hoping to deliver himself from it, he risked his life dangerously. He saved paralytics from fire, children from the bottom of ravines. The abyss spurned him; the flames spared him.

Time did not allay his suffering. It became intolerable; he resolved to die.

One day, when he was by a spring, as he was leaning over to judge the water's depth, he saw below him an emaciated old man, with a white beard and a look so piteous that it was impossible for him to hold back his tears. The other wept also. Not recognizing this face, Julian vaguely remembered a face like it. He uttered a cry; it was his father. And he thought no more of killing himself.

So, under the weight of his memories, he traveled through many lands, and came one day to a river, the crossing of which was dangerous because of its current and because there was a wide stretch of slime along its banks. No one for a long time had dared to cross it.

An old boat, buried at the stern, raised its bow among

the reeds. Julian, on examining it, found a pair of oars; and the idea came to him of employing his life in the service of others.

He began by building on the shore a sort of pier that would make it possible to go out to the channel of the river. He broke his nails moving large stones, which he held against his stomach while carrying them. He slipped in the slime, he sank in it, and he nearly perished several times.

Then he repaired the boat with pieces of driftwood and built himself a hut with clay and tree trunks.

The ferry service having been heard of, travelers appeared. They summoned him from the other side by waving flags; Julian would hastily jump into his boat. It was very heavy, and they weighed it down with all sorts of baggage and freight, not to mention the beasts of burden, which added to the difficulty of passage by kicking in terror. He asked nothing for his labor; some gave him leftover victuals they took from their sacks or worn clothing they no longer needed. The more brutish shouted coarse blasphemies at him. Julian reproved them gently, and they retorted with curses. He was happy to bless them.

A small table, a stool, a bed of dead leaves, and three clay cups—that was all his furniture. Two holes in the wall served as windows. On one side, as far as the eye could see, there stretched an arid plain, spotted here and there with ghostly ponds; and in front of him the great river rolled its greenish waters. In the spring, the damp soil gave forth a decaying odor. Later, violent winds swirled dust in the air. It penetrated everywhere, muddied the water, got into the mouth. A little later, there were clouds of mosquitoes, whose buzzing and stinging ceased neither day nor night. Then followed terrible cold, which hardened everything like rock and aroused a mad longing to eat meat.

Months slipped by when Julian did not see a living soul. Many times he closed his eyes and tried to recall the days of his youth. The courtyard of a castle would appear, with greyhounds on the stone steps, footmen in the armory, and, under a trellis of vines, a blond lad between an old man dressed in furs and a lady wearing a tall coif. Then suddenly, the two corpses would be there. Julian would throw himself face down on his bed and repeat, sobbing, "Oh! My poor father and mother!" And he would fall into a stupor, but the ghastly dreams continued.

One night, when he was sleeping, he thought he heard someone calling to him. He listened attentively but could only hear the lashing of the waves.

But the same voice repeated, "Julian!"

It was coming from the other side of the river, which seemed to him strange, in view of the width of the river.

A third time, someone called, "Julian!"

And the loud voice had the ring of a church bell.

Julian lit his lantern and went outside the hut. A violent wind was blowing. The pitch blackness was pierced here and there by the whiteness of the rolling waves.

After a moment's hesitation, Julian unfastened the moorings. Instantly the water became calm, the boat glided across to the other side where a man was waiting.

He was wrapped in a tattered cloth, and his face was like a plaster mask with his eyes redder than coals. When Julian approached with raised lantern, he saw that the man was covered with hideous leprosy; yet there was in his posture a kingly majesty.

As soon as he entered the boat, it began to sink rapidly, borne down by his weight; a jolt brought it to the surface again, and Julian began to row.

With each stroke of the oars, the current raised the bow. The water, blacker than ink, lashed madly on both sides of the boat. It made deep furrows and swelled into mountains; and the boat rose over them, then fell into the depths, where it was whirled and tossed by the wind.

Julian bent his body, stretched his arms, and, bracing himself with his feet, threw himself back with a twist to get more power. The hail stung his hands, the rain drenched his back, the fierce winds took his breath, and he stopped rowing. Then the boat was carried adrift. But knowing that this passage was of great importance, an order he must not disobey, he plied his oars once more, and the squealing of the oarlocks was heard through the roaring of the storm.

The little lantern burned in the bow. Flying birds dimmed its light now and then. But always he could see the burning eyes of the Leper who stood at the stern, immobile as a pillar.

And the passage lasted a long time, a very long time!

When they had reached the hut, Julian shut the door, and he saw the Leper sitting on the stool. The kind of shroud he wore had fallen to his hips; and his shoulders, his chest, his skinny arms, were covered by splotches of scaly pustules. Deep wrinkles furrowed his brow. Like a skeleton he had a hole in place of his nose, and his bluish lips exhaled a breath as thick as fog and nauseous.

"I am hungry!" he said.

Julian gave him what he had—an old piece of bacon and crusts of black bread.

When these had been eaten, the table, the plate, and the handle of the knife bore the same spots that could be seen on the traveler's body.

Then he said, "I am thirsty!"

Julian went to fetch his pitcher; and as he took it, it gave forth an aroma that delighted his heart and his nostrils. It was wine! What luck! But the Leper held out his hand and, with one draught, emptied the pitcher.

Next he said, "I am cold!"

Julian, with his candle, lighted a bundle of bracken in the middle of the cabin.

The Leper went to warm himself by it; and, as he crouched on his heels, every limb shook. Weakened as he was, his eyes dulled; his ulcerous sores oozed, and, in a barely audible voice, he murmured, "Thy bed!"

Julian helped him gently to drag himself to it and spread over him the sail from his boat.

The Leper moaned. The corners of his mouth drooped, his teeth showed, a quickening rattle shook his chest, and his stomach hollowed to his spine with his every breath.

Then he closed his eyes.

"It is like ice in my bones! Come close to me!"

And Julian, lifting the sail, lay down on the dead leaves beside him.

The Leper turned his head.

"Undress, that I may have the warmth of thy body!"

Julian took off his clothing; then, as naked as on the day of his birth, he lay down on the bed again. He felt the skin of the Leper touching his thigh colder than a serpent and as rough as a file.

Julian tried to hearten him, and the other replied, panting, "Ah, I am dying! . . . Come closer, warm me! Not with thy hands! No, with thy whole body!"

Julian stretched himself out, mouth to mouth, breast to breast.

Then the Leper embraced him, and his eyes suddenly sparkled like stars; his hair was long like the rays of the sun; the breath from his nostrils had the fragrance of roses; a cloud of incense rose from the hearth, and the waves chanted. Meanwhile, a transport of delight, a super-human joy, descended like a flood into Julian's enraptured soul; and he whose arms still enfolded him grew and grew until his head and feet touched the two walls of the hut. The roof flew off, the firmament opened—and Julian ascended toward the blue expanses, face to face with Our Lord Jesus, who bore him to Heaven.

And that is the story of St. Julian the Hospitaler, more or less as it is found on the stained-glass windows of a church in my own province.

Herodias

1

The citadel of Machaerus rose east of the Dead Sea
on a cone-shaped basalt peak; it was girded by four deep
valleys, one on each side, one in front, and one beyond it.
Houses were huddled against its base inside an encircling
wall that followed the undulations of the uneven ground.
A zigzag road, hewn through the rock, linked the town to
the fortress, whose ramparts were a hundred and twenty
cubits high with many angles. Battlements topped the sides,
and, here and there, towers, like diadems in this crown
of stone, commanded the abyss.

Inside there was a palace, ornamented with porticoes.
Its roof was a terrace around which ran a balustrade of
sycamore wood. Atop the balustrade, poles had been set
at intervals for stretching an awning.

One morning, before dawn, the Tetrarch Herod Antipas
came to lean on the balustrade. He gazed over the landscape.

The mountains, immediately beneath him, were beginning to reveal their crests, but their massive bulk was
still in shadow at the bottom of the chasm. A mist, hanging part way down the mountain sides, parted, and the
outlines of the Dead Sea appeared. The dawn, breaking
behind Machaerus, irradiated a reddish light. Soon it lit
up the sandy beaches, the hills, the desert, and, far in the
distance, all the mountains about Judea, with their jagged
gray summits. En-gedi, in the center, formed a black bar;
Hebron, in the background, was rounded like a dome;
Esquol appeared dotted with pomegranate trees; Sorek,

with fields of sesame; and the tower of Antonia, with its huge cubic form, rose above Jerusalem. The Tetrarch turned to his right to gaze upon the palm trees of Jericho. He thought of the other towns of his Galilee—Capernaum, Endor, Nazareth, and Tiberias—to which perhaps he would never return again. The Jordan flowed over the barren plain, dazzling white, glistening like a blanket of snow. The lake now seemed to be of lapis lazuli. At its southern point, in the direction of Yemen, Antipas saw what he feared to see. Brown tents were pitched here and there; men with lances passed among the horses; and dying fires glittered like sparks on the ground.

These were the troops of the King of the Arabs, whose daughter he had cast aside to take Herodias, wife to one of his brothers, who was living in Italy with no pretensions to power.

Antipas was awaiting help from the Romans, and because Vitellius, Governor of Syria, was late in making his appearance, he was consumed with impatience.

Had Agrippa disparaged him in the eyes of the Emperor? Philip, his third brother, sovereign of Batanea, was secretly arming. The Jews wanted no more of Antipas' idolatrous ways, nor, indeed, any part of his rule, so that he was hesitating between two plans: to appease the Arabs or to enter into an alliance with the Parthians. On the pretext of celebrating his birthday, he had invited to a great banquet, that very day, the leaders of his troops, the stewards of his estates, and all the chief men of Galilee.

With a sharp eye he scanned all the roads. They were empty. Eagles circled above his head; all along the ramparts, soldiers were asleep against the walls. Nothing stirred inside the castle.

Suddenly, a far-off voice, rising as from the bowels of the earth, made the Tetrarch turn pale. He leaned forward to hear; it had ceased. Then it rose again, and he clapped his hands and called, "Mannaeus! Mannaeus!"

At once there appeared a man, naked to the waist, like the masseurs at baths. He was very tall, old, and lean; he wore at his hip a sword in a bronze sheath. His hair, being gathered back by a comb, made his forehead look higher than it was. A drowsiness dulled his eyes, but his teeth sparkled, and his toes rested lightly on the flagstones; his whole body had the suppleness of a monkey, and his face the passiveness of a mummy.

"Where is he?" asked the Tetrarch.

Pointing with his thumb to an object behind them, Mannaeus replied, "Still there!"

"I thought I heard him."

And Antipas, heaving a great sigh of relief, inquired after Iaokanann, the same man whom the Latins called St. John the Baptist. He asked if those two men who had been admitted by special favor to his dungeon some months before had been seen again; and whether, since then, the reasons for their coming had been learned.

Mannaeus replied, "They exchanged some mysterious words with Iaokanann, like thieves when they meet at crossroads in the night. Then they went off toward upper Galilee, announcing that they would bear great tidings."

Antipas hung his head, then in a terrified tone he said, "Guard him! Guard him! And let no one enter! Secure the door! Cover the hole! No one must even suspect that he is alive!"

But Mannaeus had carried out these orders before they were given; for Iaokanann was a Jew, and like all Samaritans, he hated the Jews.

Their temple at Garizim, intended by Moses to be the center of Israel, existed no longer, not since the reign of King Hyrcanus; and the Temple at Jerusalem maddened them as an outrage, as a monument to injustice. Mannaeus had forced his way into it to defile the altar with dead men's bones. His accomplices, not as quick as he was, had been beheaded.

Mannaeus saw it in the gap between two hills, its white marble walls and the golden slats of its roof flashing in the sun. It was like a luminous mountain—something super-human, overwhelming in its magnificence and pride.

Then he extended his arms toward Sion and, standing erect, with his head thrown back and his fists clenched, he cursed it, believing his words had some strange efficacious power.

Antipas listened without appearing to be shocked.

The Samaritan then spoke again, "At times he is excited, he longs to escape, he hopes for deliverance. Other times, he seems lethargic like some sick animal; or else, I see him pacing in the darkness repeating to himself, 'What does it matter? That He may increase, I must decrease!' "

Antipas and Mannaeus looked at each other. But the Tetrarch was weary of reflection.

All the mountains about him, like tiers of huge petrified waves, the black chasms on the sides of the cliffs, the immensity of the blue sky, the sudden burst of day, the depth of the abysses, troubled him. A feeling of melancholy swept over him at this spectacle in the desert, where the upheavals of the earth had made configurations of amphitheaters and ruined palaces. The hot wind brought an odor of sulphur, the exhalation of those two accursed cities, buried beneath the banks of the sea with its heavy water. These signs of an immortal fury unsettled his thoughts; and he stood there, with his elbows resting on the balustrade, staring, his hands holding his temples. Someone touched him. He turned around. It was Herodias.

She was wrapped in a long, thin purple robe that fell to her sandals. She had come from her chamber in haste, and wore neither necklaces nor earrings; a tress of her black hair fell over one shoulder and buried itself between her breasts. Her nostrils, which were excessively arched, quivered; a joyous expression of triumph lighted her face; and in a loud voice, tugging at the Tetrarch's arm, she said, "Caesar favors us! Agrippa is in prison!"

"Who told you so?"

"I know it!" She added, "It is because he wanted too much to see Caius emperor!"

While living off their charity, Agrippa had schemed for the title of king, which, like him, they coveted. But in the future, no more fear!—"The dungeons of Tiberius are difficult to open, and sometimes life is not sure therein!"

Antipas understood her; and, though she was Agrippa's

sister, her wicked conniving seemed to him justified. Such murders were consequences of the state of affairs—fatalities common in royal families. In Herod's, people had stopped counting them.

Then she laid bare her strategy: how clients had been bought, how letters were uncovered, how spies had been stationed at every door, and how she had succeeded in seducing Eutyches, the informer.

"I spared no effort! For you, have I not done more? . . . I have abandoned my daughter!"

After her divorce, she had left her child in Rome, hoping to have others by the Tetrarch. Never had she spoken about her. He wondered why this outburst of tenderness.

The awning had been unfolded, and large cushions were brought hastily to them. Herodias sank down upon them and wept, turning her back to Antipas. Then she passed her hand over her eyes and said that she did not wish to think about it anymore; that she was happy; and she recalled to him their chats in the atrium, their meetings at the baths, their walks along the Via Sacra, and the evening spent in the great villas, by some murmuring fountain, or under archways of flowers, facing the Roman campagna. She was gazing at him as she used to do, rubbing herself against his breast, with coaxing gestures.—He pushed her away. The love she was trying to rekindle was now too far spent. All his misfortunes had flowed from it, for the war had been going on now for twelve years. It had aged the Tetrarch. Under his somber toga with its violet border, his shoulders were stooped. His white hair blended with his beard, and the sun, shining through the awning, bathed his troubled brow with light. Herodias' brow too was wrinkled. Face to face, they studied each other sullenly.

The mountain roads began to teem with people. Herdsmen were driving their cattle, children were pulling donkeys, stablemen were leading horses. Those who were coming down from the heights above Machaerus disappeared behind the castle; others were climbing the ravine on the opposite side, and, having reached the town, were unloading their baggage in the courtyards. These were the Tetrarch's purveyors, and servants arriving ahead of his guests.

But at the foot of the terrace, to the left, appeared an Essene, barefooted and wearing a white robe; his air was stoical. Mannaeus, from the right, rushed toward him, brandishing his cutlass.

Herodias cried out, "Kill him!"

"Halt!" said the Tetrarch.

Mannaeus stood still; the other did, too. Then they drew back, each by a different stairway, walking backward, not taking their eyes off each other.

"I know him!" said Herodias. "His name is Phanuel, and he wants to see Iaokanann, since you were blind enough to spare his life!"

Antipas objected, saying that one day Iaokanann might be of some use. His attacks against Jerusalem would win the Jews to their side.

"No!" she said, "they accept any master and are not capable of establishing a fatherland!" As for him who stirred up the people with hopes, cherished since the time of Nehemiah, the best policy was to suppress him.

In the Tetrarch's opinion, there was no need for haste. Iaokanann dangerous? Nonsense! He pretended to scoff at the idea.

Said Herodias, "Be still!" Then she retold the tale of her humiliation: "One day, on my way to Gilead to gather balsam, people by the riverbank were putting on their clothes. On a hillock, nearby, a man was speaking. His loins were girt with camel's skin, and his head resembled that of a lion. As soon as he espied me, he hurled at me all the maledictions of the prophets. His eyes blazed with anger, his voice roared; he raised his arms as if to bring down the thunder! It was impossible to flee! The wheels of my chariot were in sand up to the axles; but I walked away slowly, concealing myself under my cloak, numbed by these insults that fell like the rain of a thunderstorm."

Iaokanann had disturbed her manner of thinking and living.

When they had seized him and tied him with cords, the soldiers were ordered to stab him if he resisted; but he was submissive. They had infested his prison with serpents; these had died!

The futility of these tricks exasperated Herodias. Besides, what was the reason for this war against her? What had he to gain by it? His discourses, delivered to the crowds, had spread and were circulating; she heard them everywhere; they filled the air. Against armies she would have been more courageous. But this intangible force, more pernicious than the sword, was overpowering. She walked back and forth on the terrace, livid with rage, lacking words to express the emotions that choked her.

She thought, too, that the Tetrarch, yielding to public opinion, would perhaps take a notion to cast her aside. Then all would be lost! From childhood she had nurtured the dream of a great empire. It was to attain one that she had left her first husband, and had married this one, who, she now thought, had deceived her.

"I gathered strong support when I entered your family!"

"It is as good as yours," rejoined the Tetrarch simply.

Herodias felt the priestly and royal blood of her ancestors boiling in her veins.

"But your grandfather was a sweeper in the temple of Ascalon! The others were shepherds, bandits, caravan chiefs—a horde dependent upon Judah from the time of King David! All my ancestors have conquered yours! The first of the Maccabees drove you from Hebron; Hyrcanus ordered that you be circumcised!" And exuding a patricians's scorn for a plebeian, Jacob's hate for Edom, she reproached him for his indifference to the outrages heaped upon him, for his softness toward the Pharisees, who betrayed him, for his cowardice toward the people, who hated him. "You are like them, confess it! And you long for the Arab girl who dances around the stones! Take her again! Go, live with her, in her tent! Eat her bread cooked in the ashes; drink the curdled milk of her sheep! Kiss her blue cheeks! And forget me!"

The Tetrarch was no longer listening. He was gazing

upon the roof of a house, on which there was a young maiden with an old woman who was holding a parasol by its reed handle as long as a fisherman's rod. In the middle of the rug, there lay open a large traveling basket. Girdles, veils, pendants, jewelry overflowed from it in confusion. Every so often, the young girl bent over these things and shook them in the air. She was dressed like the Roman women, in a fluted tunic, with a peplum hung with green tassels. Blue ribbons bound her hair, which, doubtless, was heavy, for from time to time she would raise her hand to it. The shade of the parasol above her half-concealed her as she walked. Two or three times Antipas caught a glimpse of her slender neck, the slant of her eye, the corner of her small mouth. But he could see her whole figure, from the hips to the neck, as she bent over and straightened up again with buoyant grace. He watched for the repetition of these movements and he panted more heavily; flames burned in his eyes. Herodias was observing him.

"Who is she?" he asked.

Herodias replied that she had no idea, and, suddenly appeased, she left.

Some Galileans—the chief scribe, the chief of the pastures, the manager of the salt mines, and a Babylonian Jew, who commanded his horsemen—awaited the Tetrarch under the porticoes. All greeted him with cheers. Then he disappeared into his inner chambers.

Phanuel suddenly appeared at a corner in the passageway.

"Ah, you again? No doubt you come to see Iaokanann?"

"And to see you! I have something of great importance to tell you."

And, following closely behind Antipas, he entered a dark room. Light filtered through the latticework that extended the length of the room under the cornice. The walls were painted a deep red, almost black. At the end of the room stood an ebony bed, with cords of oxskin. A gold buckler above gleamed like a sun.

Antipas walked the length of the room and lay down on the bed.

Phanuel remained standing. He raised his arm and, as if inspired, said, "The Most High sends at times one of His sons. Iaokanann is one. If you do him violence, you will be punished."

"It is he who persecutes me!" cried Antipas. "He asked of me an impossible act. Since then, he has rent me to pieces. In the beginning, I was not severe with him! He even sent men from Machaerus to throw my provinces into confusion. Woe to him! Since he attacks me, I must defend myself!"

"His anger is too violent," replied Phanuel. "But no matter. You must free him."

"One does not loose mad beasts!" said the Tetrarch.

"Have no fear," answered the Essene. "He will go among the Arabs, the Gauls, the Scythians. His work must spread to the ends of the earth!"

Antipas seemed lost in a vision.

"His power is strong! . . . In spite of myself, I love him."

"Then let him go free!"

The Tetrarch shook his head. He feared Herodias, Mannaeus, and the unknown.

Phanuel tried to persuade him, alleging, as a guaranty of his plans, that the Essenes would submit to the kings. People respected these poor men, clothed in flax, unbending under torture, who read the future in the stars.

Antipas recalled Phanuel's words of a little while before.

"What is this matter which you said was of such importance?"

A Negro appeared. His body was white with dust. He gasped and could only say, "Vitellius!"

"What? He is coming?"

"I saw him. He will be here within three hours."

The curtains in the corridors fluttered as if by the wind. A hum filled the castle; it was the tumult of people running about, of furniture being moved, of silver plate falling to the floor; and, from the tops of the towers, trumpets sounded, to warn the scattered slaves.

2

The ramparts were swarming with people when Vitellius, leaning on the arm of his interpreter, entered the courtyard. He was followed by a huge red litter adorned with feathers and mirrors. He was wearing the toga, the laticlave, the laced boots of a consul, and was surrounded by lictors.

They stood their twelve fasces against the door—staves bound together by a strap with an ax in the center. Then all trembled before the majesty of the Roman people.

The litter, which required eight men to manage, stopped. There descended a youth, with a fat belly, a pimply face, and pearls on his fingers. They offered him a cupful of wine and some spices. He drank and asked for another draught.

The Tetrarch, who had fallen at the feet of the Proconsul, was grieved, he said, that he had not been apprised sooner of this favor accorded by his presence. Otherwise, he would have ordered along the roads everything to assure the comfort of the Vitellii, who were descended from the goddess Vitellia. A road leading from Janiculum to the sea still bore their name. Quaestorships and consulships were beyond counting in the family; and, as for Lucius, now his guest, they owed thanks to him as the conqueror of the Cliti and as the father of this young Aulus, who seemed to be returning to his own domain, since the Orient was the fatherland of the gods. These extravagant compliments were expressed in Latin. Vitellius accepted them indifferently.

He replied that the great Herod was enough to make a nation glorious. The Athenians had made him the supervisor of the Olympic games. He had constructed temples in honor of Augustus, had been patient, ingenious, awesome, and always loyal to the Caesars.

Between the columns, with their bronze capitals, Herodias was seen, advancing with the poise of an empress, amidst women and eunuchs carrying burning perfumes on silver trays.

The Proconsul took three steps to meet her; and she saluted him, bowing her head, and exclaimed, "What good fortune that henceforth Agrippa, the enemy of Tiberius, is powerless to do any harm!"

The Proconsul knew nothing of the event. Herodias seemed to him dangerous; and when Antipas had sworn that he would do anything for the Emperor, Vitellius interjected, "Even to the detriment of others?"

He had taken hostages from the King of the Parthians, and the Emperor no longer remembered it; but Antipas, who was present at the conference and had wanted to appear important, had instantly dispatched the news. From this ensued a profound hate, and delays in sending help.

The Tetrarch stammered. But Aulus said, laughing, "Don't worry; I will protect you!"

The Proconsul pretended not to hear. The father's fortunes depended upon the son's debasement; and this flower from the mire of Caprae had procured for Vitellius such considerable benefits that every attention was paid him, though, as a poisonous flower, he was distrusted.

A tumult rose beneath the gate. A file of white mules was led in. Mounted on them were personages in priestly garb. They were Sadducees and Pharisees, come to Machaerus for the same ambitious reasons; the first wanted to obtain and to control the rites of sacrifice; the latter, to hold on to them. Their faces were grave, especially those of the Pharisees, who were hostile to Rome and to the Tetrarch. The skirts of their tunics hampered them in the crowd; and on their heads their tiaras tottered above bands of parchment covered with writing.

Almost at the same time soldiers of the vanguard arrived. They had put their shields in sacks as a precaution against the dust; and behind them followed Marcellus, lieutenant of the Proconsul, with publicans carrying wooden tablets under their arms.

Antipas introduced the chief men of his entourage: Tolmai, Kanthera, Sehon, Ammonius of Alexandria, who purchased asphalt for him, Naaman, captain of his lighter armed troops, and Jacim the Babylonian.

Vitellius, who had noticed Mannaeus, inquired, "That one over there, what does he do?"

The Tetrarch, with a gesture, gave him to understand that he was the executioner.

Then he presented the Sadducees. Jonathas, a small man of easy carriage, who spoke Greek, begged the master to honor them with a visit to Jerusalem. He replied he probably would.

Eleazar, with hooked nose and long beard, demanded for the Pharisees the cloak of the high priest, kept in the tower of Antonia by the civil authorities.

Then the Galileans roundly denounced Pontius Pilate. On the occasion of some madman who was seeking David's golden vessels in a cave, near Samaria, Pontius Pilate had killed some of the inhabitants. They all spoke at once, Mannaeus more violently than the others. Vitellius declared the culprits would be punished.

Loud cries broke out in front of the porticoes, where the soldiers had hung their shields. When the coverings were removed, there was seen in the engravings the image of Caesar. This, for the Jews, was idolatry. Antipas harangued them, while Vitellius, from an elevated seat in the colonnade, was astonished by the heat of their fury. Tiberius had been right to exile four hundred of them to Sardinia. But in their own country they were powerful, and he ordered the bucklers to be removed.

Then they surrounded the Proconsul, imploring a redress of their grievances, privileges, and charity. They rent their garments. People trampled one another; and, to make room, slaves struck right and left with sticks. Those nearest the gate went down to the road; others came up it; they surged back; two currents met in a mass of men that moved back and forth, contained by the enclosing walls.

Vitellius asked why there were so many people. Antipas explained that his birthday was the reason. He pointed out several of his people, who were leaning over the battlements, lowering huge baskets of meats, fruits, vegetables, antelopes and storks, large bluefish, grapes, melons, pomegranates arranged like pyramids. Aulus could not restrain himself. He rushed for the kitchens, impelled by a gluttony that was to amaze the world.

Passing by a cave, he took note of cooking pots like cuirasses. Vitellius approached to look at them and demanded that these underground rooms of the fortress be opened for him.

These rooms were hewn out of rock, with high vaulted ceilings, supported by pillars evenly spaced. The first room contained old armor; but the second was crammed with pikes, all their points protruding from a bouquet of plumes. The third seemed to be tapestried with reed matting, so many slender arrows were there standing up straight side by side. Scimitar blades covered the walls of the fourth room. In the middle of the fifth room, rows of helmets, with their crests, formed, as it were, a battalion of red serpents. In the sixth were to be seen only quivers; in the seventh, only military leggings; in the eighth, only armlets, in the other rooms, pitchforks, climbing irons, ladders, robes, even poles for catapults, and bells for the breastplates of dromedaries! As the mountain grew larger at its base, hollowed out inside like a beehive, under these rooms, there were others more numerous and still deeper.

Vitellius, Phineas, his interpreter, and Sisenna, the chief publican, walked through these rooms by the light of torches carried by three eunuchs.

In the shadows, they could distinguish hideous objects contrived by the barbarians: truncheons studded with nails, poisonous javelins, tongs that resembled the jaws of crocodiles. In a word, the Tetrarch possessed in Machaerus war munitions for forty thousand men.

He had gathered them anticipating that his enemies might enter into an alliance. But the Proconsul might think, or might say, that these arms were to fight against the Romans. Then Antipas would fumble for explanations; such as, that they were not his; many of them served for defense against brigands; moreover, he needed them against the Arabs; or else, they had all belonged to his father. And instead of walking behind the Proconsul, he walked ahead of him rapidly. Then he stood against one wall, which he endeavored to hide with his toga, by extending his arms apart; but the top of a door was clearly visible above his head. Vitellius noticed it and wanted to know what was within.

Only the Babylonian could open it.

"Summon the Babylonian!" ordered Vitellius.

They awaited him.

This man's father had come from the banks of the Euphrates to offer his services to the mighty Herod, with five hundred cavalrymen, to protect the eastern frontiers. After the partition of the kingdom, Jacim had remained with Philip, and now was in the service of Antipas.

He arrived, with a bow over his shoulder and a whip in his hand. Cords of many colors were bound tightly about his bandied legs. His sinewy arms issued from a sleeveless tunic, and a fur cap shaded his face; his beard was curled in ringlets.

At first he seemed not to understand the interpreter. But Vitellius shot a glance at Antipas, who immediately repeated his order. Then Jacim put both hands to the door. It slid into the wall. A waft of hot air came from the darkness. A winding path led downward. This they followed until they reached the entrance to a grotto, more extensive than the other subterranean chambers. At the extreme end there was an arch that opened over the precipice, which defended the citadel on that side. Honeysuckle, clinging fast to the wall, dropped its blossoms in the bright light of the sun. Over the ground below trickled a thread of murmuring water.

There were perhaps a hundred white horses eating barley

from a board on a level with their mouths. All had their manes painted blue, their hoofs in mittens of esparto, and their forelocks in waves, like a wig. Their very long tails swung gracefully against their legs. The Proconsul was dumb with admiration. They were marvelous beasts, as supple as serpents, as light afoot as birds.

They would bolt off with the shot of their rider's arrow, knock down men and bite them in the stomach; would extricate themselves from hard places in rocks; jump over ravines, and for a whole day could travel at a wild gallop over the plains; a word would stop them. As soon as Jacim entered, they went to him, like sheep when the shepherd appears, and stretching our their necks, they looked at him with childlike, restless eyes. From habit he uttered a deep, raucous cry that aroused their spirits. They reared, hungry for the open spaces, begging to run free.

Antipas had shut them up in this place that was especially designed for animals in case of a siege, for fear that Vitellius might lead them off.

"It is a bad stable," said the Proconsul, "and you might lose them! Count them, Sisenna!"

The publican took a tablet from his girdle, counted the horses, and wrote down the number.

The agents of the tax companies bribed the governors in order to pillage the provinces. This one, with his blinking eyes and his weasel-like jaw, sniffed about everywhere.

Finally they went up again to the courtyard.

Small round shields of bronze, set here and there in the pavement, covered the cisterns. Vitellius noticed one larger than the others, which did not ring underfoot. He struck them all in turn, then shouted, stamping on one of them, "I have it! I have it! Herod's treasure is here!"

The search for his treasure was a mania with the Romans.

The Tetrarch swore that such treasure did not exist.

But, what was there underneath?

"Oh, nothing! A man, a prisoner."

"Show him to me!" said Vitellius.

The Tetrarch did not obey; the Jews would have dis-

covered his secret. His reluctance to open the cover made
Vitellius impatient.

"Break it in!" he shouted to his lictors.

Mannaeus had guessed what was holding their attention.
When he saw the ax, he thought that they were going to
behead Iaokanann. He stopped the lictor at the first blow
on the plate and he himself inserted a kind of hook
between it and the pavement; then, stiffening his long thin
arms, he raised it gently. It fell back; everyone marveled at
the old man's strength. Beneath the wood-lined cover was
a trap door of the same dimensions. With a blow of his
fist, it split into two panels. Then they saw a hole, an
enormous pit with an unrailed staircase winding down into
it; those who leaned over the edge could make out at the
bottom something indistinct and terrifying.

A human being lay on the ground, covered with long
hair that seemed to mingle with the hair shirt that clothed
his back. He got up. His forehead touched the horizontal
bars fixed over the pit. From time to time he would disappear into the dark recesses of his cave.

The sun made the points of the tiaras and the swordhilts
glitter; it made the flagstones excessively hot; and doves,
flying from the cornices, fluttered around above the courtyard. It was the hour when Mannaeus usually threw grain
to them. He was now crouched before the Tetrarch who
was standing near Vitellius. The Galileans, priests, and
soldiers formed a half-circle behind them; all were silent,
apprehensive about what was going to happen.

First, there was a deep, cavernous sigh.

Herodias heard it at the other end of the palace. Driven
by a sort of fascination, she made her way through the
crowd; and, with one hand resting on Mannaeus' shoulder, she bent forward to listen.

A voice rose from the pit, "Woe to you, Pharisees and
Sadducees, ye brood of vipers, inflated skins, sounding
cymbals!"

They recognized the voice of Iaokanann. His name was
whispered around. Others gathered to hear.

"Woe to you, O people! Woe to you, traitors of Judah,

drunkards of Ephraim, and those who dwell in the lush valley and who stagger with the fumes of wine!

"Let them pass away like flowing waters, like the melting snail, like a woman's dead foetus which sees not the sun.

"Thou must flee, Moab, into the cypresses like sparrows, and into caves like jerboas. The gates of the fortresses shall be broken easier than nutshells, the walls shall crumble; the cities shall burn, and the scourge of the Eternal God shall not cease. He shall turn over your limbs in your blood as wool is turned in a dyer's vat. He shall tear you as a new harrow; He shall scatter all the bits of your flesh upon the mountains."

Of what conqueror was he speaking? Was it Vitellius? Only Romans could effect such extermination. Murmurs arose from the crowd. "Enough! Enough! Let him finish!"

He continued, louder still, "To the corpses of their mothers, little children shall drag themselves over ashes. You shall go at night to seek your bread among the ruins, at the risk of the sword. Jackals shall fight over your bones in the public squares, where, in the evening, old men used to talk. Your virgins, choking back their tears, shall play the lute at the stranger's banquets, and the bravest of your sons shall bend their backs under enormous weights!"

The people remembered the days of their exile and all the calamities of their history. These were the words of the prophets of old. Iaokanann now hurled them forth, like mighty blows, one after the other.

But suddenly his voice became soft, harmonious, musical. He proclaimed deliverance, glorious signs in the heavens, the time when the newborn child would put his arm into the dragon's lair; there would be gold where there was clay, and the desert would bloom like a rose. "That which is now worth sixty talents shall not cost a farthing. Fountains of milk shall gush from rocks; you shall sleep with full bellies in the wine presses! When wilt Thou come, O Thou whom I hope for? In anticipation, all peoples shall kneel and Thy dominion shall be everlasting, O Son of David."

The Tetrarch drew himself back: the existence of a Son of David was an insult to him and a threat.

Iaokanann chastised him for his kingship, saying, "There is no king but the Eternal God!" and railed against the Tetrarch for his gardens, his statues, his ivory furniture— "like the impious Ahab!"

Antipas broke the cord of the seal that hung upon his breast and hurled it into the hole, bidding the prophet to be silent.

The voice replied, "I will give voice like the bear, like a wild ass, like a woman giving birth to her child!

"Thy incest is already punished. God afflicts thee with the sterility of a mule!"

And laughter arose, like the splashing of waters.

Vitellius persisted in staying there. The interpreter, in a calm voice, repeated in the Roman tongue all the invectives that Iaokanann had bellowed in his own. The Tetrarch and Herodias were compelled to listen to them for a second time. He panted, while she gazed open-mouthed into the bottom of the pit.

This hideous-looking man threw back his head and, clutching the bars, pressed his face against them, a face that looked like a scrawny tangle of underbrush in which gleamed two coals of fire.

"Ah! It is thou, Jezebel!

"Thou hast captured his heart with the creaking of thy slipper. Thou didst neigh like a mare. Thou hast set thy bed upon the mountains to perform thy sacrifices!

"The Lord shall tear off thine earrings, thy purple robes, thy linen veils, the bracelets on thine arms, the rings on thy feet, and the little golden crescents that dangle about thy forehead. He shall take thy silver mirrors, thy fans of ostrich feathers, the soles of mother-of-pearl that give thee height, thy diamonds, the perfumes for thy hair, the painting on thy nails—all the artificial devices of thy sensuality; and there shall not be stones enough to stone thee, adulteress!"

She looked around for a defender. The Pharisees hypocritically lowered their eyes. The Sadducees turned their heads away, fearing to give offense to the Proconsul. Antipas seemed as if he were about to die.

The prophet's voice, louder and more booming, rumbled like the crashing of thunder, and, as the echo in the mountain took it up, it struck Machaerus like so many thunderbolts.

"Stretch thyself in the dust, daughter of Babylon! Grind flour! Take off thy girdle, unloose thy shoes, truss up thy robes, cross the rivers! Thy shame shall be known, thy disgrace shall be seen! Thy teeth shall be broken with all thy sobbing! The Eternal God abhors the stench of thy crimes! Accursed, O accursed one, die like a dog!"

The trapdoor was closed and the cover was lowered in place. Mannaeus was longing to strangle this Iaokanann.

Herodias disappeared. The Pharisees were scandalized. Antipas, in their midst, sought to justify himself.

"Doubtless," said Eleazar, "a man may marry his brother's wife, but Herodias was not a widow; and besides, she had a child; this is the abomination."

"Wrong, wrong!" objected Jonathas, the Sadducee. "The Law forbids these marriages without absolutely outlawing them."

"It makes no difference! People are grossly unjust to me!" said Antipas, "for, after all, Absalom slept with his father's wives, Judah with his daughter-in-law, Ammon with his sister, Lot with his daughters."

Aulus, who had been sleeping, reappeared at that moment. When he was informed of the whole affair, he sided with the Tetrarch. One ought not be disturbed by such foolish notions; and he laughed uproariously at the censure of the priests and Iaokanann's fury.

Herodias, who was standing halfway up the palace steps, turned around toward him. She said, "You are wrong, my lord! He is ordering the people not to pay taxes."

"Is that true?" questioned the publican instantly.

The replies were in the main affirmative, and the Tetrarch confirmed them.

Vitellius thought that the prisoner might escape; and, as the behavior of Antipas seemed to him equivocal, he stationed sentinels at the gates, along the walls and in the courtyard.

Then he betook himself to his rooms, accompanied by delegations of priests.

Each delegation advanced its grievances, without broaching the question of the office of high priest. All importuned him, so he dismissed them.

Jonathas left when he saw Antipas on the battlements talking with a man with long hair dressed in white—an Essene—and he was sorry that he had defended him. One thought afforded the Tetrarch consolation: Iaokanann was no longer his concern. The Romans had taken charge. What a relief!

Phanuel was walking on the path around the battlements at that moment. The Tetrarch called him and said, pointing to the soldiers, "They are stronger than I! I cannot save him and it is not my fault!"

The courtyard was empty. The slaves were resting. Against the red sky, all aflame on the horizon, the smallest objects stood out in black against it. Antipas could make out the salt mines on the farther end of the Dead Sea, but he could no longer see the tents of the Arabs. Undoubtedly they had left. The moon was rising; a feeling of calm swept over him.

Phanuel, dejected, remained with his chin upon his breast. Finally he said what he had to say.

Since the first of the month, before each dawn he had studied the heavens when the constellation of Perseus was at its zenith. Agalah was barely visible; Algol was glittering less brilliantly; Mira-Coeti had disappeared. All this augured for him the death of a man of importance, that very night, in Machaerus.

But who? Vitellius was too well guarded. They would not execute Iaokanann. "Then it is I," thought the Tetrarch.

Perhaps the Arabs would come back. The Proconsul might discover his relations with the Parthians! Hired assassins from Jerusalem were escorting the priests; likely they carried daggers under their clothing. The Tetrarch could not doubt Phanuel's learning.

He thought of appealing to Herodias. He hated her, however. But she would give him courage; moreover, all the bonds of the charm that had once bound him to her were not broken.

When he entered her room, cinnamon was smoking in a basin of porphyry; powders, unguents, fluffy fabrics like clouds, embroideries lighter than feathers were scattered about.

He did not say anything of Phanuel's prediction, nor of his own fears of the Jews and Arabs; she would have called him a coward. He spoke only about the Romans. Vitellius had confided nothing about his military plans. Antipas had supposed him to be a friend of Caius, with whom Agrippa consorted, and he himself might be sent into exile, or perhaps he would have his throat cut.

Herodias, with an air of indulgent contempt, tried to reassure him. Finally, she took from a small box a strange-looking medal, stamped with the profile of Tiberius. That would be enough to make the lictors turn pale and accusations melt away.

Antipas was touched with gratitude and asked her how she had obtained it.

"Someone gave it to me," she replied.

Opposite them, beneath a curtain, a bare arm emerged, a young, lovely arm that might have been sculptured in ivory by Polycletus. A little hesitatingly, but yet gracefully, it groped about in the air, trying to grasp a tunic left behind on a stool near the wall.

An old woman pulled back the curtain and slipped the tunic deftly through.

The Tetrarch vaguely remembered the face, but could not place it.

"Does that slave belong to you?"

"Of what concern is it to you?" answered Herodias.

The guests filled the banquet hall.

It had three naves, like a basilica, divided by pillars of algum wood, with bronze capitals covered with carvings. Two galleries with open lattice-work overhung; and a third, in gold filigree, jutted out at the end of the hall, opposite an enormous arch at the other end.

Candelabra, burning on long tables that lined the whole length of the hall, made bushes of fire. Between them sat painted pottery cups and copper dishes. Interspersed among these were bowls of snow cubes and platters of grapes. As the evening progressed, these twinkling points of light grew dim, like stars seen at night through tree branches. Through the opening of the great arch, one could see torches on the terraces of the houses, for Antipas was feasting his friends, his people, and all those who had come.

Slaves, agile as dogs, their toes covered in sandals of felt, moved about carrying dishes.

The Proconsul's table beneath the gilded tribune stood upon a dais parqueted with sycamore. Babylonian tapestries enclosed it in a kind of pavilion.

Three ivory couches, one facing the hall and one on each side, held Vitellius, his son, and Antipas; the Proconsul was near the door, to the left of it; Aulus was on the right, and the Tetrarch was in the center.

He wore a heavy black cloak, the texture of which was invisible underneath the layers of dyestuffs. He wore rouge on his cheekbones, a fan-shaped beard, and blue-powdered hair gathered together by a diadem of precious stones. Vitellius kept on his purple baldrick, which diagonally crossed his linen toga. Aulus had the sleeves of his purple robe of silk, shot with silver, tied behind his back. The ringlets of his hair were in layers, and a pendant of sapphires sparkled on his breast, full and white like a woman's. Beside him, on a mat, with legs crossed, sat a very beautiful boy, always smiling. Aulus had seen him in the kitchen and could not be without him, and having difficulty remembering his Chaldean name, called him simply the "Asiatic." From time to time, he stretched himself on his triclinium. Then his bare feet would dominate the assemblage.

On one side there were the priests and officers of Antipas, Jerusalemites, and the chief men of the Greek cities; and, below the Pronconsul: Marcellus with the publicans, some friends of the Tetrarch, the notables of Cana, Ptolemais, and Jericho; then, arranged helter-skelter, were the mountaineers from Lebanon and old soldiers of Herod: twelve Thracians, a Gaul, two Germans, gazelle hunters, Idumean shepherds, the sultan of Palmyra, and sailors from Eziongeber. Each had before him a cake of soft paste on which to wipe his fingers; and their arms, stretched out like vultures' necks, seized olives, pistachios, and almonds. Beneath their floral crowns all their faces were gay and joyous.

The Pharisees had spurned them as Roman indecencies. They shuddered when they were sprinkled with galburnum and incense, a mixture reserved for use in the Temple. Aulus rubbed his armpits with it; and Antipas promised him a whole load of it, with three baskets of genuine balsam which had made Cleopatra covet Palestine.

A captain, just arrived from his garrison at Tiberias, had placed himself behind Antipas to tell him of some extraordinary events. But the Tetrarch's attention was divided between the Proconsul and what was being said at the nearby tables.

They were talking about Iaokanann and other people like him; Simon of Gittoy cleansed sins with fire. A certain Jesus . . .

"The worst of all," cried Eleazar. "An infamous mountebank!"

In a rage, a man back of the Tetrarch rose, white as the hem of his chlamys. He came down from the platform and challenged these statements of the Pharisee, saying, "All lies! Jesus does work miracles!"

Antipas wanted to see some. "You should have brought Him with you! Tell us more."

Then he recounted how he, Jacob, having a sick daughter, had betaken himself to Capernaum, to implore the Master to heal her. The Master had replied, "Return home, she is cured!" And he had found her in the doorway, having left her bed when the dial marked the third hour, the very moment when he had accosted Jesus.

Of course, objected the Pharisees, there were devices and potent herbs! Even here, in Machaerus, one could find the *baaras,* which makes men invulnerable; but to heal without seeing or touching the person was impossible unless Jesus consorted with demons.

And the friends of Antipas, the chief men of Galilee, repeated, shaking their heads, "Demons, evidently."

Jacob, standing between their table and the table of the priests, kept proudly but humbly silent. They called upon him to speak: "Explain his power!"

He bent his shoulders and said, in a whisper, slowly, as if afraid of himself, "You know not then that He is the Messiah?"

All the priests looked at each other, and Vitellius asked the meaning of the word. His interpreter hesitated a minute before answering. Then, continuing, he explained that they called by that name a liberator who would bring to them the enjoyment of all the goods of this world and power over all peoples. Some even maintained that two were to be expected. The first would be vanquished by Gog and Magog, demons of the North; but the other would exterminate the Prince of Evil. He asserted that for centuries they had awaited His coming every minute.

The priests consulted one another, and it was Eleazar who spoke. First of all, he said, the Messiah would be a son of David, and not the son of a carpenter. He would confirm the Law, this Nazarene attacks it; and, a stronger argument, He was to be heralded by the coming of Elias.

Jacob replied, "But Elias *has* come!"

"Elias! Elias!" repeated the crowd, even to the farthest end of the banquet hall.

Each, in his imagination, saw an old man beneath a flock of ravens, lightning illuminating an altar, and idolatrous pontiffs being cast into torrents. The women in the tribunes thought of the widow of Sarepta.

Jacob wearied himself repeating that he knew him! He had seen him, and the people had seen him, too!

"His name?"

Then with all his strength he cried out, "Iaokanann!"

Antipas fell back as if smitten full in the chest. The Sadducees pounced upon Jacob. Eleazar shouted to make himself heard.

When silence was established, he draped his cloak about him and, like a judge, asked questions.

"Since the prophet is dead. . . ."

Murmurs interrupted him. It was believed that Elias had only disappeared.

He grew impatient with the crowd and continued his line of interrogation.

"You think that he has come to life again?"

"And why not?" demanded Jacob.

The Sadducees shrugged their shoulders; Jonathas opened wide his beady eyes and forced a clownish laugh. Nothing could be more absurd than the body's claim to immortality; and, for the benefit of the Proconsul, he declaimed a verse from a contemporary poet:

> *After death the body grows not,*
> *Seems not to endure.*

But Aulus was leaning over the edge of his triclinium, his brow beaded with sweat, his face green, his hands on his stomach.

The Sadducees pretended some deep emotion—the following day the office of high priest was given back to them. Antipas made a show of despair; Vitellius remained unperturbed. Nevertheless, his anxiety was sorely felt; with his son he stood to lose his fortune.

Aulus had no sooner finished vomiting than he wanted to eat again.

"Give me some marble dust, schist from Naxos, sea water, anything! Supposing I took a bath?"

He chewed some snow, then, hesitating between a Commagene stew and uncooked blackbirds, he decided upon honeyed gourds. The Asiatic studied him; this capacity for gulping food denoted a prodigious being and one of a superior race.

They served bull kidneys, dormice, nightingales, and minced meat in vine leaves; while the priests discussed the question of resurrection. Ammonius, disciple of Philo the Platonist, thought them stupid and said so to some Greeks who were poking fun at oracles. Marcellus and Jacob had come together. The first was telling the second of the happiness he had experienced during his baptism by Mithra, and Jacob was urging him to follow Jesus. Palm and tamarisk wines, wines from Safet and Byblos, flowed from pitchers into bowls, from bowls into cups, from cups down parched gullets. There was much gossiping, the tongues of all were loosened. Jacim, although a Jew, no longer concealed his great admiration of the planets. A merchant from Aphaka flabbergasted the nomads by detailing the wonders of the Temple of Hieropolis; and they asked how much a pilgrimage there would cost. Others held fast to the religious beliefs of their birth. A German, almost blind, sang a hymn praising that promontory of Scandinavia where the gods are said to have appeared with halos about their faces; and people from Sichem refused to eat turtle-doves, out of deference for the dove Azima.

Many stood talking in the middle of the hall; the vapor of their breath, together with the smoke from the candelabra, made a kind of fog in the air. Phanuel moved along the walls. He had just been studying the heavens again, but he did not go up to the Tetrarch, for fear of being smudged by the oil, which, for an Essene, would be a great pollution.

Sounds of banging against the gate of the castle were heard.

It was generally known now that Iaokanann was being held prisoner there. Men with torches were wending their way up the pathway; a black mass swarmed in the ravine; and every once in a while they would cry out, "Iaokanann! Iaokanann!"

"He is upsetting everything!" said Jonathas.

"We won't have any money if he continues," added the Pharisees, hurling forth more recriminations.

"Protect us!"

"Let us finish him off!"

"You are giving up your religion!"

"Sacrilegious, like the Herods!"

"But less so than you!" retorted Antipas. "It was my father who erected your temple!"

Then the Pharisees, the sons of the proscribed, the partisans of Matathias, accused the Tetrarch of the crimes of his family.

They had weak and evil-looking hands, pointed skulls, bristling beards on faces with flat noses, large round eyes, and the look of bulldogs. A dozen of them, scribes and servants of the priests, fed upon the refuse of sacrifices, rushed as far as the foot of the dais; and with knives they threatened Antipas, who harangued them while the Sadducees looked on and only half-heartedly came to his defense. He caught sight of Mannaeus and motioned him to go away; Vitellius indicated by his expression that these things did not concern him.

The Pharisees, who remained on their couches, worked themselves into a demoniacal rage. They smashed the plates before them. They had been served with a stew of wild ass, a favorite dish of Maecenas, which was an unclean meat.

Aulus railed at them about the ass's head, which they held in honor, it was said, and spouted other sarcasms about their aversion for pork. Doubtless it was because that fat beast had slain their Bacchus; and they had liked their wine too much ever since a golden vine had been found in the Temple.

The priests did not understand his words. Phineas, a Galilean by birth, refused to translate them. Thereupon, Aulus became raging mad; all the more so, as the Asiatic, overcome with fright, had disappeared. The repast displeased him; the dishes served were mediocre and insufficiently garnished! He grew calmer when he saw a fatty dish made from the tails of Syrian sheep.

The character of the Jews seemed obnoxious to Vitellius. Their god could well be Moloch, whose altars he had encountered on the road. He remembered the sacrifices of children, and the story of the man they were mysteriously fattening. His Latin heart revolted in disgust against their intolerance, their rage against images, their inflexibility of character. The Proconsul wanted to leave, but Aulus refused.

His robe had fallen to his waist; he lay behind a heap of food, too full to indulge himself more, but too obstinate to leave.

The excitement of the people increased. They abandoned themselves to devising schemes for independence. They recalled the glory that was Israel's and how all the conquerors had been successively punished: Antigonus, Crassus, Varus. . . .

"Scoundrels," said the Proconsul; for he understood Syriac; his interpreter only served to give him time to frame his answers.

Antipas, trembling, very quickly drew out the Emperor's medallion and, looking at it, held it with the image up.

Suddenly, the panels of the golden tribune were opened; and in the brightness of candlelight, between her slaves and amid wreaths of anemone, Herodias appeared—crowned with an Assyrian miter held in place by chin straps; her hair fell in ringlets over a purple peplum, slit up the length of the sleeves. Framed in the doorway, between two stone monsters similar to those that guard the treasure of the Atrides, she looked like Cybele flanked by her lions; and from the top of the high balustrade, above

Antipas, with a patera in her hand, she cried out, "Long live Caesar!"

Vitellius, Antipas, and the priests echoed her homage.

But there came from the back of the hall a hum of surprise and admiration. A young girl had just come in.

Through a bluish veil draped over her head and breast, you could see the arch of her eyes, her agatelike ear lobes, the whiteness of her skin. A square piece of shot silk concealed her shoulders and was fastened to her loins by a jeweled girdle. Her black undergarment was embroidered with mandrakes. Indolently she tapped on the floor with her small shoes, decorated with hummingbirds' down.

When she reached the dais, she threw back her veil. It seemed as if Herodias had returned just as she was in her youth. Then the girl began to dance.

Her feet moved in front of each other to the beat of the flute and a pair of castanets. Her rounded arms seemed to be calling for someone who was forever fleeing. She was pursuing him, lighter than a butterfly, like an inquisitive Psyche, like a wandering spirit. She seemed as if she were about to fly away.

The melancholy strains of smaller flutes followed the castanets. Dejection had followed hope. Her poses conveyed the meaning of sighs, and her whole person, such a languor that no one knew whether she was weeping for a god or dying in his caresses. Her eyes were half-closed; she wriggled her hips, and when she rolled her belly like undulating waves, her breasts would quiver. Her face remained impassive, but her feet did not stop.

Vitellius likened her to Mnester, the pantomimist. Aulus was still vomiting. The Tetrarch was lost in a dream and he no longer was thinking of Herodias. He thought he saw her near the Sadducees. Then the vision faded away.

It was not a vision. It was Salome, Herodias' daughter, whom Herodias had had trained, far away from Machaerus, and whom now the Tetrarch loved. It was an excellent idea. She was sure of him now!

Then it was love's heat that begged satisfaction. Salome danced like the Indian priestesses, like the Nubian girls of the cataracts, like the Bacchantes of Lydia. She lolled from side to side as a flower blown in the storm. The diamond pendants in her ears leaped and glittered; the garment on her back shone in the shimmering light. It seemed as if sparks shot forth from her arms, her feet, her clothes, setting all the men afire. A harp made music and the crowd applauded. By spreading her legs apart, but without bending her knees, she stooped so low that her chin touched the floor; and the abstemious nomads, the Roman soldiers, experts in debauchery, the greedy publicans, the old priests, embittered by long disputes, all with their nostrils dilating, quivered with a fiery longing.

Then she danced around Antipas' table in a passionate dance, turning like the magic wheel of witches; and, in a voice broken with sobs of lust, he said to her, "Come! Come here!" She went on dancing; the drums beat as if they would burst, and the crowd roared. But the Tetrarch shouted louder, "Come here! Come here! Capernaum shall be yours! The plain of Tiberias! All my citadels! Half my kingdom!"

She threw herself on her hands, heels in the air, and thus circled the dais like a huge beetle. Then suddenly she stopped.

Her neck and spine were at right angles. The sheaths of color that wrapped her legs fell over her shoulders like a rainbow, framing her face, a cubit from the ground. Her lips were painted, her eyebrows were deep black, her eyes were almost terrifying. Beads of perspiration shone on her forehead like drops on some piece of white marble.

She did not speak. They looked at each other.

A snapping of fingers was heard in the tribune. She went up, reappeared; and lisping a little, she uttered these words with a childish air: "I want you to give me on a platter the head . . ." She had forgotten the name, but began again, smiling, "the head of Iaokanann!"

The Tetrarch fell back, aghast.

He was bound by his word, and the people were waiting. But the death that had been predicted for him, should it befall another, perhaps his own might be averted. If Iaokanann were really Elias, he could escape it; and if he were not, the murder would be of no importance.

Mannaeus was beside him, and knew his intention.

Vitellius called the man back to give him the password for the guards at the pit.

It was a relief. In a moment, all would be over!

But Mannaeus was not very prompt at his task.

He came back, but greatly upset.

For forty years he had been the executioner. It was he who had drowned Aristobulus, strangled Alexander, burned alive Matathias, beheaded Zosimus, Pappus, Joseph, and Antipater; yet he dared not kill Iaokanann! His teeth chattered and his whole body was trembling.

He had seen the Great Angel of the Samaritans in front of the pit, all covered with eyes, and brandishing a huge sword, red and jagged like a flame. Two soldiers whom he had with him as witnesses could testify.

But they had seen nothing, excepting a Jewish captain, who had rushed at them, and who now no longer was alive!

The fury of Herodias burst forth in a torrent of vulgar and cutting insults. She tore her nails on the grating of the tribune, and the two sculptured lions seemed to be biting at her shoulders and roaring like her.

Antipas imitated her, and so did the priests, the soldiers, the Pharisees, everyone crying for revenge; the others were indignant that their pleasure was being delayed.

Mannaeus left, hiding his face.

The guests found the time even longer than the first time. They were getting bored.

Suddenly, the sound of footsteps echoed in the corridors. The suspense was unbearable.

The head was brought in; Mannaeus was holding it by the hair, at arm's length, proud of the applause that was given.

When he had laid it on a platter, he offered it to Salome. Very nimbly she mounted the tribune; several minutes later, the head was brought back by the same old woman whom the Tetrarch had noticed that morning on the house roof, and later had seen in Herodias' chamber.

He stepped back so as not to look at it. Vitellius glanced at it indifferently.

Mannaeus went down from the dais and displayed it to the Roman captains, then to everyone who was eating on that side of the hall.

They examined it.

The sharp blade of the instrument had slanted downward and had cut into the jaw. The corners of the mouth were convulsively drawn. Blood, already clotted, sprinkled the beard. The closed eyelids were as pale as shells as the candelabra shone upon them.

The head reached the table of the priests. A Pharisee turned it over curiously; and Mannaeus, having turned it right side up again, placed it before Aulus, who was awakened by it. Through their parted lids, the dead eyes of the one and the dulled eyes of the other seemed to speak to each other.

Then Mannaeus presented it to Antipas. Tears streamed down the cheeks of the Tetrarch.

The torches were extinguished. The guests left; and now there was no one in the hall but Antipas, his hands against his temples, still gazing at the severed head, while Phanuel, standing in the center of the great nave, mumbled prayers with his arms outstretched.

At the moment when the sun was rising, two men, previously sent out by Iaokanann, returned with the long-awaited answer.

They confided it to Phanuel, who was enraptured by it.

Then he showed them the lamentable object on the platter, amidst the remnants of the feast. One of the men said to him, "Be consoled! He has gone down to the dead to announce the Christ!"

The Essene now understood the meaning of these words, "I must decrease that He may increase."

Then all three, carrying the head of Iaokanann in turn, as it was very heavy, went away in the direction of Galilee.

SELECTED BIBLIOGRAPHY

OTHER WORKS BY FLAUBERT

Memoires d'un Fou, 1838
Madame Bovary, 1857   Novel
Salammbô, 1862   Novel
The Sentimental Education, 1869   Novel
The Temptation of St. Anthony, 1874   Novel
Bouvard and Pécuchet, 1881   Unfinished Novel
Correspondence, 1925-1928, 1954

SELECTED BIOGRAPHY AND CRITICISM

Bart, Benjamin F. *Flaubert's Landscape Description.* Ann Arbor: University of Michigan Press; London: Oxford University Press, 1957.

Giraud, Raymond. *The Unheroic Hero in the Novels of Stendhal, Balzac and Flaubert.* New Brunswick, N. J.: Rutgers University Press, 1956.

James, Henry. *Future of the Novel.* New York: Alfred A. Knopf (Vintage Books), 1959.

Shanks, Lewis Piaget. *Flaubert's Youth: 1821-1845.* Baltimore: Johns Hopkins Press, 1927.

Spencer, Philip. *Flaubert: A Biography.* New York: Grove Press, 1953. London: Faber & Faber, 1952.

Steegmuller, Francis. *Flaubert and Madame Bovary: A Double Portrait.* New York: Farrar, Straus & Young, 1951; London: William Collins Sons & Co., 1947.

———— (tr. and ed.). *Selected Letters of Gustave Flaubert.* New York: Farrar, Straus & Cudahy; London: Hamish Hamilton, 1954.

SIGNET CLASSICS by French Authors

PERE GORIOT *by Honoré de Balzac*

The 19th century French writer's interpretation of the King Lear theme. New translation with Afterword by Henry Reed.
(#CP139—60¢)

CANDIDE, ZADIG and Selected Stories *by Voltaire*

Voltaire satirizes with ruthless wit the social, religious, and human vanities of his day in sixteen biting stories. A new translation with an Introduction by Donald Frame. (#CD35—50¢)

ADOLPHE AND THE RED NOTE-BOOK *by Benjamin Constant*

By the close friend of Mme. de Stael, this 18th century French novel is the story of a young man's passion for a woman with whom he can never be happy, *Adolphe* translated by Carl Wildman; *The Red Notebook* translated by Norman Cameron. Introduction by Harold Nicolson. (#CD1—50¢)

LES LIAISONS DANGEREUSES *by Choderlos de Laclos*

The diabolical story of the systematic corruption of the innocent by two partners in jealousy exposes the tragic folly of hyper-rationality in 18th century France. Translated by Richard Aldington with a Foreword by Harry Levin. (#CT127—75¢)

ATALA AND RENE *by Francois René de Chateaubriand*

Two charming romantic tales, whose heroes are American Indians, by the French author who has been called "the true founder of Romanticism in France." Newly translated, with a Foreword by Walter J. Cobb. (#CD103—50¢)

MANON LESCAUT *by Abbé Prevost*

The first modern "novel of passion" on which the operas of Massenet and Puccini are based. Newly translated with an Introduction by Donald Frame. (#CP96—60¢)

THE PRINCESS OF CLEVES *by Mme. de Lafayette*

A profound and delicate psychological novel about a woman involved in a triangle. Newly translated with a Foreword by Walter J. Cobb. (#CD89—50¢)